PRA[ISE]

"Reminiscent of Ka[fka...] cascade of surreal absurdities, but rather than giving in to despair, confused protagonist invites the reader to be like him and surrender to the chaos and embrace the adventure: truly a message for our times!"
- Derek Hanebury, Best Selling Co-Author of *Both Sides Now*

"Bit of wry and sparkling writing from Huei Lin… in the tradition of William Sydney Porter. Lin's Lotus-eating protagonist bumps up against a sacred cow, somehow coming out ahead in a semi-successful search for enlightenment. We should all be so disenchanted. More to come from this promising writer, we think." **- Jacqueline Carmichael, author of *Tweets from the Trenches***

"*Coda* is a riveting series of short stories that render us disoriented by their compelling surrealism and intoxicated by their gritty inner worlds. Lin's imagination is the richest of his generation, offering prose worth imbibing. You will be left thirsting for more." **- William Tappertit, Poet**

"Certainly, thought provoking and borderline radical… The premise and context of twisting the usual to the unusual was a very good touch that made me keep on reading." **- Don Tecson, Host of *The Wave***

"As a 'writer' it was eye-opening and thought-provoking to read this… about the tags we are given because of what we do or don't do… Thoroughly enjoyable, well-written." **- Joan Donaldson-Yarmey, Best Selling Author**

"Written with humour, the author balances the pursuit of spiritual wisdom with a Jewish-grandmotherly type of advice on daily living. Self-deprecating fun with a spiritual twist."
- Vicki Drybrough, Best Selling Co-Author of *Both Sides Now*

"Author Huei Lin shines a humorous light on the parallel between a writer's struggle with creativity and spiritual peace. The 'eat meat don't eat meat' school of enlightenment at its best." **– Libbie Morin, Best Selling Co-Author of *Both Sides Now***

"This is a thought-provoking poke at our modern world with its thin-skinned veneer. Will we remember valuable lessons or will we continue to blind ourselves to our realities? The ending packs a punch… a brilliant contemporary romp." **- Gail Morton, Author of *Two Weeks With Charlie***

CODA

A short story collection by Huei Lin

RCN Media Publishing

Coda © 2020 by Huei Lin & RCN Media

All rights reserved. No part of this publication may be reproduced, distributed, or transmitted in any form or by any means, including photocopying, recording, or other electronic or mechanical methods, without the prior written permission of the publisher, except in the case of brief quotations embodied in critical reviews and certain other noncommercial uses permitted by copyright law. For permission requests, write to the publisher, addressed "Attention: Permissions Coordinator," at the address below.

All pictures and artwork are created and copyrighted by Huei Lin, all rights reserved.

First Edition: March 2021

RCN Media was founded in 2015 by Colton Nelson. It is a publishing company for adult, young adult and children's books. The RCN Media logo is © 2015 by Colton Nelson & RCN Media. If you require bulk orders of an issue with an RCN Media contact, feel free to contact them with the info below. Special discounts are available on quantity purchases by corporations, associations, and others. For details, contact the publisher at the email address below.

Cover artwork © 2021 by RCN Media & Huei Lin

Artwork created and adapted by Huei Lin and Sahara von Hattenberger © 2021 by Huei Lin & RCN Media. Some rights reserved.

Colton Nelson was the head of production and is the promoter for this novel. For any comments or to contact the author you can reach them through him (contact below) or you can contact RCN Media.

Contact:
www.rcn.media
(250) 206 0356
nelsoncolton16@gmail.com (subject: "Coda by Huei Lin")

1   3   5   7   9   8   6   4   2   0

King of Dhamma originally published as a stand a lone short story July 2020 by RCN Media. Printed with person in this collection by the publisher. King of Dhamma © July 2020 by RCN Media.

Pulse originally published as a stand a lone short story November 2020 by RCN Media. Printed with person in this collection by the publisher. Pulse © November 2020 by RCN Media.

The Courier originally published as a stand a lone short story February 2021 by RCN Media. Printed with person in this collection by the publisher. The Courier © February 2021 RCN Media.

Available in eBook, Paperback and Audiobook

TABLE OF CONTENTS

King of Dhamma 10

Pulse 24

2007 40

Shanghai Sylvia 72

The Courier 94

Flesh and Blood 106

Coda 120

4' 33" 180

To Julie, an original downtown woman

We miss your kindness, and your inspiration

–

To Tatiana, a no-nonsense artist of the first order

We miss your music, and your candor

KING OF DHAMMA

"May all beings be happy."

The venerable S. N. Goenka squinted. Then he launched into a mesmerizing chant, closing out our seventh day of silent meditation. He was our teacher: the world's eminent and tireless champion of Vipassana, a warmhearted old man with a mission. Under his tutelage, a forlorn cast of down-and-outs had assembled in this pastoral getaway and committed themselves to ten full days of noble asceticism. After confiscating our belongings for the duration of the retreat, our instructors then presented us with a stark list of prohibitions to observe during our stay. Among the banned activities: speaking, making eye contact, eating meat, killing, consuming intoxicants, reading, writing, masturbating, and fraternizing with members of the opposite sex.

We rose at 4 AM and winnowed the rest of the day away chasing the dissolution of the self, or a cathartic moment. Nothing but this, twelve hours a day. Punctuated by two very light vegetarian meals that made the most of brown rice and miso soup. Sleep, it turns out, was a precious commodity in perpetually short supply. Crammed in a room with twenty other devotees, we moaned in our creaky beds and waited for the wakeup bells to sound.

The one highlight of our day was the evening discourse. Each night we congregated in a small room to receive S. N. Goenka's wisdom, which he dispensed with saintly calm and deadpan wit. But he wasn't in the room with us. Actually, he was no longer with us, and hadn't been for more than a decade: the late Goenka had moved on to greener pastures in the cycle of samsara, leaving us with mere video recordings of his lectures. Shot on VHS, these videos served as a kind of communion: the shoddy camerawork, paired with Goenka's droll anecdotes, was a welcome dose of slapstick philosophy. Huddled around an old TV monitor, we hung on to every word. It was the S. N. Goenka Show.

"Breathe. Breathe with a calm and equanimous mind."

On this particular night, I had forgotten my hair elastic in the room after the evening discourse. While everyone else dozed fitfully in their beds, I tiptoed back to the lecture room. Failing to locate the light switch, I knelt on my hands and knees, feeling around in the dark for my hairband. I didn't find it, but something else happened. The TV screen turned itself on.

The room was suddenly aglow, the TV monitor crackling drunkenly. The image stuttered for a few moments, as if something were trying to rip through the curtain of pixels and materialize onscreen. Then, he was there. The distinguished S. N. Goenka— smiling at me with his trademark equanimity. The sudden burst of light from the TV startled me. Figuring that the VCR must have been activated somehow, I grabbed the remote control from beside the screen. But before I could turn off the TV, S. N. Goenka deigned to speak.

"Hello there. Shouldn't you be in bed?"

I dropped the remote and shrank back against the wall, cowering speechlessly. S. N. Goenka eyed me with ruthless compassion.

"You seem frightened, good sir. Don't be scared. I don't often get to chat with anyone, on account of my being quite dead."

When I'd told my friends that I planned to attend a meditation course, they'd immediately tried to dissuade me. They warned that nothing would come of such masochism — aside from, possibly, some very unpleasant hallucinations. At the time, I had blithely shrugged off their concerns. Now, I was talking to a dead man.

"You know— after I died, I was reincarnated as a cat somewhere in Manhattan, in New York City. Not a bad life, but somehow less than satisfactory when it comes to sophisticated thought. That's why I keep a signpost to my previous vessel here, in this realm."

I gurgled something unintelligible.

"Well are you going to say something? How are you liking bootcamp? How do you like the food? Pretty bleak, eh?"

S. N. Goenka then proceeded to pick his nose, examine the booger, and flick it onto the floor.

"I'll be honest with you. I've never seen such a sorry pack of dunces in my entire life. Hopeless, every single one of you. I don't know why you're wasting your time here at this New Age gang bang. Here's some real advice for your problems: marijuana and fried chicken."

His thick Indian accent— which generally enhanced the rhetorical content of his lectures— now seemed somehow incongruous with the astonishing utterances coming out of his mouth. Presently, he reached over to his left, out of the frame. When his hand came back into view, it was holding what looked like a greasy drumstick. Into this, S. N. Goenka sank his saintly teeth with the frantic pleasure of an addict. The camera quickly zoomed in, moronically drawing the viewer's attention to his ravenous jowls. It was like a bad KFC commercial.

At this point, I found my voice again.

"So... you're not a vegetarian?"

S. N. Goenka snorted between bites of chicken that seemed way too large.

"Hell no! Who do you think I am? You suckers can starve yourselves silly with those twigs and leaves they serve, but I'll stick to real food, thank you very much."

He drove this point home with another mouthful of flesh, more copious than the last. Before I could respond to this frankly breathtaking disclosure, S. N. Goenka burst into spontaneous chant, his gullet still stuffed with fried chicken. It was much louder than the prerecorded version at the end of his lectures. Every few seconds a piece of meat would get lodged in his throat, setting off a violent fit of coughing before he resumed his thundering incantation. Eventually, he ran out of chicken.

"Ahem. Now, it's your turn. Young man, who the hell are you? What's your deal?"

The amazing thing was that throughout this decidedly irreverent binge, S. N. Goenka never lost his composure. His kindly gaze never drifted from the camera lens. I swallowed.

"Well, uh, I'm a writer. But I've been feeling a lot of anxiety recently because I can't seem to finish a story and..."

His eyes glazing over, S. N Goenka gnawed at the chicken bone and snapped it in half, sucking greedily at the marrow before tossing the pieces on the floor. Then he wiped his hands on his robe and reached out of the frame. When his hand reappeared, it was holding what was unmistakably a joint. He stuck it in his mouth, retrieved a lighter from offscreen, and lit up. The camera zoomed in, then out, then back in. The esteemed Goenka took a pull, coughed violently, then let out a sigh of deep contentment.

"Ahhhhh, that's better. Please, continue."

Somehow, I continued.

"Yes well, I guess you could say that I'm at a sort of crossroads.

I'm not really happy with my work, and I'm not sure what I want to do with my life. I'm trying to write a novel..."

S. N. Goenka interrupted me.

"A novel about what?"

"I guess it's mostly about being young and disillusioned in the modern world."

The illustrious Goenka groaned.

"Stop right there. I haven't read your book yet, but I'm already bored. Don't you have anything else to talk about? You millennials are such a drag. Always on about being lost and confused, or stricken with guilt because your Chinese grandmother doesn't understand you."

Beneath a cemetery somewhere in suburban Virginia, my own Chinese grandmother gave a gargle of approval from the other side. S. N. Goenka took the opportunity to remove the joint out of his mouth and hold it in front of him, right up against the screen.

"Want to get in on this?"

He winked.

"I am joking. You look like you could use some, however."

He laughed a thick, belly laugh while the camera went in for an unflattering close-up of his chin. The preeminent Goenka blew a cloud of smoke toward the camera lens and plowed ahead.

"So what do you think of the chicks here? Assuming of course, that you're a *cis-gendered hetero*, as you young people say these days."

"What? I mean, we're not allowed to talk to anyone, so..."

"Sex. Now there's a hook I can get behind. Why don't you write about that?"

"Well actually, I do explore modern sexuality and the internet..."

S. N. Goenka again reached for something offscreen and the camera panned in the opposite direction, practically cutting him out of the frame. When it re-centered, he was holding a magazine. It was an old issue of Penthouse from 1985. He flipped through it and squealed with delight, turning it around and holding up a centerfold spread for my pleasure. Comfortably seated on a gaudy chaise lounge, a serene-looking Goenka beamed at the camera with two pouting, svelte models perched on either side. A headline read: "Equanimous Desire: A Silent Romp with the King of Dhamma." I couldn't make out the text of the article underneath, but it hardly mattered.

"I can't stand these 'journalists'— they make me out to be some kind of nymphomaniac. I simply teach dhamma, and sometimes the females want a photo with me. That's it. I'm not some sicko bastard like 'guru' Bikram. Hot yoga is a total farce, anyway. It's just an excuse to undress and fill a room with sweaty bodies."

He paused, and put the magazine on the floor. "But back to your book."

"Yes?"

"I just have one piece of advice for you."

"Okay?"

"Write about whatever you want, but don't call yourself a 'writer'. Once you start thinking of yourself as a 'writer', you're finished."

"Oh."

"Take me, for instance. I'm not a guru, meditation czar, expert, yogi— these terms are just conveniences to make it easier for people to understand the world. I've been busting my ass to get people to meditate— that's it. Just a regular guy who's gone down the rabbit hole with this meditation thing."

The joint, which had been burning through at a startling clip, appeared to be done. S. N. Goenka took one last hit and then flicked the spent end onto the ground. He continued, visibly blazed but still present.

"Remember this. People who feel the need to call themselves 'artists', 'leaders', 'mixologists', 'dim sum specialists'— they will never be great. Possibly good, but never great. It's the difference between Salieri and Mozart."

I didn't catch the reference, but I could vaguely imagine what Goenka was getting at. The camera zoomed out, and then in slightly. It occurred to me that I should try to get some sleep; in any case, maybe this whole spectacle was simply the result of prolonged sensory deprivation. Yawning, I informed the renowned S. N. Goenka that this was all very interesting but that I would be retiring for the night. Goenka nodded and raised his hand magnanimously.

"That is all fine and good, sir. Sleep well, with a calm and equanimous mind."

As I stood up to leave, I asked him if I should turn off the TV on my way out. S. N. Goenka waved me away.

"No, no. I'll turn this contraption off myself."

The TV screen went dark, noiselessly. I wondered if this was because it had, in fact, never been on in the first place.

I ended up going back every night after that.

Each time, S. N. Goenka would appear just as before and expound upon such hard-hitting topics as polyamory ("The more the merrier!"), psychotropic drugs ("Why do you think I got into meditation in the first place?"), and religion ("Hahahahaha!"), always with a joint or cigarette in hand. This apparition bore an exact physical likeness to the real S. N. Goenka— the sober voice of enlightenment— but departed from him in all other respects. This thing was Goenka on the loose, Goenka at large; a rogue shaman, free from the shackles of orthodoxy. He talked endlessly. And we always managed to get on the topic of my book.

"Don't try so hard to write. Nothing kills good writing like words. Words are death. It's the space between the words that you should be interested in."

Slowly, things were starting to make sense.

"During the evening discourses I'm always telling you: when you get down to the level of elementary consciousness, you realize that there is no self. Now, the same applies to writing. There's no writer, do you understand? The novel is already there. You just have to invite it in— and that's where you need a pliable mind, and some introspection. I know some herbs that can help you with that..."

This went on until the final night of the retreat. After ten grueling days of self-actualizing, it was time to go at last. The next morning, I would leave this place forever and go back to my plodding, uncertain routine. Kneeling before the TV screen for the last time, I thought of something.

"Do you... do you talk to any of the other students? You know, after class?"

The honorable S. N. Goenka took a deep drag on his cigarette and smiled.

"Each and every one of them. Not always through the TV screen, but yes."

I suppose this shouldn't have surprised me. For someone capable of communicating from beyond the grave— through a TV screen, no less— engaging in dozens of simultaneous conversations was surely child's play. But nonetheless, this revelation left me feeling jealous and territorial.

"Really? But I haven't heard anything from anyone else..."

S. N. Goenka coughed phlegmatically and ashed his cigarette onto a hypothetical tray offscreen, followed by a dizzying camera maneuver up to his forehead, down to his lips, then out again until his torso was perfectly centered in the frame.

"When you leave this place, you won't remember these conversations. What you've learned from me— that is to say, him— will remain with you, but these clandestine sessions will disappear from your memory completely. It is my gift to you, to everyone who passes through. And once they finish the course, they will forget."

This was distressing news, and I told him so. I begged him to reconsider. Losing these nights, I told him, would rob me of the most compelling material to ever come my way. As a writer, holding these dialogues in my heart would give me an edge over the other chroniclers— perhaps affording my work a level of insight that would take the literary world by storm. I waxed indignant and morose, droning obnoxiously about phantoms and the caprice of inspiration. S. N. Goenka listened to my sycophantic bluster with a smile, but did not budge. In the end, I succeeded only in exposing the depth of my own conceit.

A long silence hung in the space between me and an undefined netherworld inhabited by spectral entities such as the late S. N. Goenka, broken only by the sound of my own heartbeat. Finally, we said our farewells.

"Well, goodbye then."

"Goodbye, good sir. May your mind be peaceful and equanimous. May all beings be happy."

Then, he added:

"Send me a copy of your book once it's published. It may be unreadable, but send it anyway."

And that was it.

The next day, I woke up with no recollection of the "after hours" discourses. I felt fresh and full of purpose. I took the first bus to the train station, and then took the train back to the city. Happy, for once, to return to my shabby apartment, I immediately started writing. Within a few days, a manuscript of value was taking shape.

I ascribed this surge in productivity to my time spent in spiritual sequestration, gushing to my friends and family about the benefits of meditation and the value of ascetic restraint. They nodded politely, with strained enthusiasm, but expressed genuine surprise at my uncharacteristically positive demeanor. I wrote late into the night, drinking cups of green tea and blasting the complete Yellow Magic Orchestra catalogue in order to stay awake. Finally, it was done. Upon publication, my debut effort made a splash, commanding public and critical acclaim. I remembered nothing of my evenings with the "other" Goenka.

Until I saw him again.

Years later, walking to the train on Baxter Street in lower Manhattan, New York, I stepped into a neighborhood joint called Sun Sai Gai Restaurant for a quick snack and a respite from the sun. The place was overrun with tourists, construction workers, mid-west hipsters, and me. Unfinished chapters of a new novel wrote and rewrote themselves in my mind while I stuffed myself with chicken, rice, and jasmine tea. Something out there was stirring— I didn't know it then, but we were about to get pulverized by a mysterious new pathogen and an unprecedented political realignment in its wake. But none of that mattered right now. I closed my eyes. An equanimous moment in a sensual world.

When I left the restaurant, I heard an unusually loud meow coming from above. I looked up and locked eyes with a black cat perched on the fire escape. Distinguished old eyes. We stared at each other for a full ten seconds while the city convulsed around us, staggering along a rusty conveyer belt in the wrong direction. The fragrance of oil and death kissed us good day, and a car full of students slammed into a taxi. Old scores were left unsettled, left to macerate in the shadows. The cat blinked, once. And I remembered.

PULSE

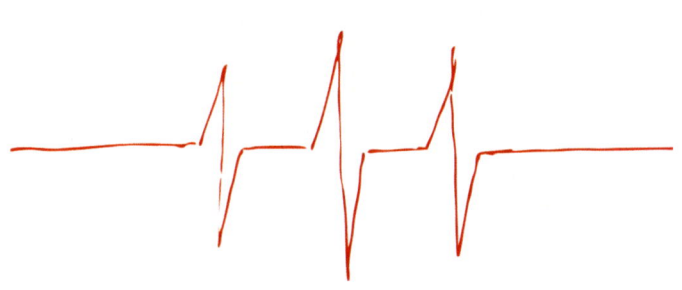

Everyone's born with something missing. For some people, it's intelligence; for others, they enter this world without charisma or empathy. There are those who are born without sight, without irony, without ambition, without sentimentality. Others still are born without brains; they usually don't last very long. Some are born with missing limbs— pinkies, arms, legs.

The first time I saw someone with only four fingers on one hand, I was in a bodega with my mother on the Lower East Side. I was ten years old, and he was at least five times that. My mother was busy hunting down bargain rolls of toilet paper, and I'd wandered off into a different aisle to browse the potato chips. The man appeared, seemingly from nowhere, examining a bag of sour cream and onion-flavored Lay's. His hair was stringy and grey, like old tangled fishing line from the pier. A flotsam head. He was hunched over, and muttering to himself. Without looking up, he said:

"There are no onions in this. And there is sure as hell, in my opinion, no goddamn sour cream either."

Then he grabbed the bag of chips and turned to me, dangling it with one hand. He was slightly cross eyed.

"No sour cream."

I bit my lip and didn't say a word. Those happened to be my favorite chips.

"Have you ever seen someone with missing fingers before?"

I shook my head. My mother was miles away in the other aisle, picking through toilet paper.

"Here, let me show you."

Still dangling the potato chips, the man took his other hand and stretched it in front of me, revealing a calloused row of appendages. His thumb was missing. I stared, mesmerized, as the man flexed his four remaining fingers and began to cackle.

"Bet you never saw *that* before, did you?"

I shook my head. Meanwhile, my mother had tracked down the best deal on toilet paper and was scouring the aisles to retrieve me. When she saw the man with four fingers, her face hardened into a streetwise leer. She strode over to the potato chip rack, grabbed my arm, and yanked me away from my companion. As we were leaving the shop, I looked back. The man was holding a different bag of chips and shaking his head, muttering, "Jalapeño, my ass," under his breath.

*

I was born without a heart. This is not an unheard of— or especially unique— circumstance: in fact, millions of babies are born without hearts every year. Which usually means they're dead on arrival, circumventing the transience of life altogether. Or, they go straight to hell. It depends who you ask.

I still don't have a heart. Not even a bionic one. I'm fast approaching midlife, and I haven't keeled over just yet. When my mother gave birth, the doctors couldn't figure out why I was still alive. I had no pulse, and an x-ray scan confirmed their diagnosis: my heart was missing. They gravely informed my mother that even if I wasn't dead yet, I most certainly would be by the end of the day. My parents were devastated, of course. The hospital agreed to keep me under observation for twenty-four hours— mostly for the sake of my stricken family. My father went outside to smoke a cigarette, I'm told, while my mother wept into her sterilized pillow and refused to speak. My grandparents were also present. The mood was, needless to say, funereal.

Except, I refused to die.

Despite the hospital's dire— and entirely justified— prognosis, my vital signs improved dramatically in the days following my birth. One day became two, then three. I still had no pulse. After about a week, the attending physicians were forced to concede that I was, in all other respects, a normal baby. I became a minor celebrity. For a mercifully brief period, medical professionals and tabloid journalists swarmed the hospital to get a better look at me, the baby with no heart. The airwaves were set ablaze with speculations and pseudoscientific conjecture. And yet, nobody could explain my condition. The hospital became a kind of circus, my mother's resting quarters overwhelmed by unscrupulous marketeers from the sensationalist columns. My family quickly grew fed-up with the unwanted attention and withdrew into obscurity. The case went cold, and public interest waned. Dismissed as hearsay by the mainstream media and the medical establishment, the incident was quietly forgotten. It survived only as a byline in the pages of the city's most disreputable papers, languishing in the good company of UFO sightings, celebrity doppelgängers, and right-wing conspiracies. As far as my parents were concerned, this was the best possible outcome. They were just happy to have me alive.

*

Living without a heart is nothing special. I don't require any prosthetic implants or chemical regulators to manage my condition. As far as I can tell, my life is indistinguishable from anyone else's. I'm living in a small apartment on East Broadway, trying to figure out what to do with myself. As it happens, this isn't going so well. To be honest, I can barely figure out what to eat for dinner— much less find my calling and transcend the banality of this fleeting, material existence on Earth. My "best years" have been a bewildering slow burn, and I keep waiting for something to happen. Something to vindicate thirty-five years of borrowed time and make light of my improbable escape from oblivion. It's as if the ledgers of death sorted me into the wrong category, and my survival is simply a clerical oversight. Once they catch the person responsible for this administrative blunder, it's curtains for me. It's only a matter of time before they figure it out and hastily correct their error. As such, I expect to keel over at any moment. But so far, I'm still here.

I've long given up consulting medical experts. They will almost certainly fail to solve the mystery of my condition, and I don't relish the thought of another media frenzy— or the ambitious researchers clamoring for access to what is a confirmed medical miracle. I just want to be left in peace so I can decide what to have for dinner. Tonight, it's Hainanese Chicken Rice from a takeout shop under the Manhattan Bridge.

Only one person ever offered a coherent explanation for my missing heart. Years ago, I had a one-night stand with someone I met at a movie theater. The movie was called "Belladonna of Sadness" — a violent, erotic animated feature by a Japanese production house and based on a French story from the 19th Century. The lush, psychedelic illustrations cut incongruously against the gratuitous rape scenes that recalled the debauchery of the Marquis de Sade. I left the theater feeling both impressed and deeply rattled. I imagine that if I'd been born with a heart, it would have been racing. I loitered on the street for a minute while I collected myself, and tried to decide where to eat dinner. Just when I'd settled on pizza, the girl appeared. She was wearing a long trench coat and had her brown hair tied up in a loose knot. I looked up, and she smiled at me.

"Hey, you were in the movie just now, right?"

"Yep. Pretty, well, *disturbing*. Great animation though."

"すごい！"

"Excuse me?"

"Oh, I'm taking a Japanese class right now. That's why I wanted to see the movie."

"Right on."

The girl continued.

"I was sitting behind you."

"Oh yeah?"

"I'm Shelly."

"Xuan. Nice to meet you."

"Do you want to get dinner?"

I was surprised by her forwardness, at first. But then again, I thought, it's 2018.

"Oh, sure. I was just going to get some pizza..."

"Are you alone?"

"Um, yep. Yeah, I'm alone."

"Pizza sounds great. Do you know a place?"

We walked over to a dollar pizza joint on Orchard Street near Delancey. I ordered two plain slices and a bottle of orange juice. The girl ordered four slices, two plain and two with green peppers. We set our trays down on a wobbly table near the bathroom. The table was covered with someone else's crumbs and a couple of receipts. I conscientiously swept these offending particles into the palm of my hand with my napkin and threw them in the trash. Then I rejoined my companion, who had already polished off an entire slice of pizza.

We talked about nothing in particular for a few minutes, during which time I learned that she hailed from a farm in Wyoming and currently lived in East Williamsburg. Nothing new, there.

At some point, I noticed that one of her hands only had four fingers. It was missing a thumb— just like the man in the bodega. She must have noticed me staring, because between large bites of pizza she took her hand— the one with only four fingers— and brandished it sardonically.

"It didn't get cut off by a tractor, if that's what you're thinking. I was born this way."

She immediately started humming the lyrics to "Born This Way", by Lady Gaga. An employee at the pizzeria, who had just come out of the bathroom, smiled at us and started humming along approvingly. All we needed was a karaoke machine, a disco ball, and some alcohol to upgrade this outing into a truly wild night.

"Are you grossed out?"

"What? No, of course not."

"It's okay to be grossed out, you know."

"No, no, seriously. Actually, this isn't the first time I've met someone with missing fingers."

"Really?"

I told her about the man in the bodega. She chewed thoughtfully on her green pepper pizza, eyeing me with genuine interest.

"Huh. That guy's probably dead now."

"Because he had missing fingers?"

"No, because he sounds like a crazy bum."

Just then, the radio came on and "Born This Way" started blasting from the house speakers. Behind the counter, the same pizzeria employee gave a big thumbs up and sprinkled some cheese onto a freshly rolled pie.

"Is it, you know, a turnoff? Me only having four fingers on one hand?"

"What? No, no, it's totally fine. It's definitely, you know, *different*, but it honestly doesn't make much difference to me."

"Other kids used to bully me in school, all the time. One of them even spit on my face in the yard during recess — can you believe that?"

"Wow."

"I punched one of them in the mouth, one time. I'd had enough, you know? It was this guy— Mike LeBoeuf. A total dumbass. He kept saying stuff like 'hey girl, how do you give a hand job with only four fingers? Maybe you could try it on me.' This went on for months. One day I just turned around and punched him in the face. It hurt my hand— especially since I used my, you know, the handicapped one — but he wasn't expecting it at all and I ended up breaking his nose. I got in sooo much trouble with the school, you wouldn't believe it. My parents were the worst. 'Why in hell would you do that? That boy just *likes* you is all, are you stupid or something?' To which I said, that's bullshit. And very soon after that, I left that shit town and came here. I haven't been back since."

"That's some story."

"Not really. It's just the truth."

She flexed her fingers— all four of them— and tapped the table in time to "Born This Way."

"Would *you* go for a girl with a missing thumb?"

I hastily changed the subject.

"You know, I don't tell most people this— but I was born with something missing, too."

"No kidding? You're disfigured too?"

"Yeah. The truth is, I was born without a heart."

"Without a *heart?*"

"I know, it's hard to explain. But I don't have a heart, even now."

I placed my hand over my chest.

"There's nothing in here. The entire organ is missing."

"You're kidding."

"No, I swear."

I held my arm out in front of me and placed two of my fingers on my wrist by way of a demonstration.

"No pulse."

The girl stared at my arm, then reached across the table and put her hand on my wrist. I felt my face grow warm, but my pulse was, naturally, unaffected. She adjusted her grip on my wrist, trying to detect signs of a nonexistent heartbeat. Her fingers were lean and angular; full of dexterity. On her, four fingers looked completely natural; to think of her hand as "handicapped" seemed crude and ignorant. I saw the guy behind the pizza counter grinning at me, nodding ecstatically as he spun a ball of dough on the countertop. This moment seemed to last for days. Eventually, the girl removed her hand and took another bite of green pepper pizza.

"So. You weren't kidding."

"Nope."

"But how is that possible? How are you not dead? You don't have, you know, an artificial heart?"

"My parents wanted me to get one when I was little. They were convinced that I would die at any moment. But I seemed fine, and the operation would have been this huge ordeal. And they didn't like telling people about my condition— not even doctors— because whenever they did, people would go berserk trying to 'study' me. It was too stressful, so they just let it go. I'm still here, and nothing else about me seems to be wrong."

"That's incredible."

"I don't like telling people about it. I don't want anyone to get any ideas, or to think I'm a freak."

"But you really don't feel *anything* differently?"

"Well, I wouldn't know. I've never had a heart. Maybe I *do* feel differently, and I just don't realize it."

The girl was lost in thought, playing with the crust from her pizzas. I drank my orange juice without further comment. Suddenly, she spoke up.

"I have a theory."

"A theory?"

"About you."

"Really."

She cleared her throat.

"Isn't it weird how words have all of these layered meanings? The word 'dream', for example, can mean dreams— as in *dreams*, when you sleep— or aspirations, like your dreams in life. *Or*, they're like delusions. When someone says 'in your dreams', they mean that you're crazy or unrealistic in your expectations. See what I mean?"

"Yeah, that's a good point. It's interesting how language evolved this way. And most people aren't even aware of these nuances— they just pull out these words without thinking, take them for granted."

"Exactly."

The pizza was extra greasy tonight, so I downed the rest of my orange juice and considered getting another.

"The word 'heart' is like that too. It refers to the blood pumping organ, a physical object. Or, it refers to a figurative bundle of emotions to do with love, hate, sensitivity, all that. It's not a 'real' thing— it's just an emotional interface. Know what I mean?"

"Yeah, very true."

"Well, my theory is... my theory is that you were born without a physical heart, but an idea took its place and does the job just fine."

"An idea?"

"The figurative heart. The metaphor. The intangible source of real empathy and intuition."

Feeling thirsty, I got up and grabbed another bottle of orange juice from the fridge. Even after four slices of pizza, the girl didn't order anything to drink.

"That's a cool idea, but I mean, I should still be dead."

"But you're not."

"Certainly not."

"And the doctors haven't figured it out?"

"No, not yet."

"Then my theory is as good as anyone else's. 'Where the conceit of reality ends, truth gushes forth from the wild gullies of dreams'."

"Who said *that?*"

"I did."

"Huh."

I offered her a sip of orange juice, but she shook her head.

"But I'm not the only one with empathy and intuition. Plenty of people have that— don't you think *most* people have that? It's nothing special."

"Everyone is made of flesh and blood. But maybe this is a temporary state of affairs. Maybe we're supposed to evolve beyond our physical bodies. Some day, we may exist as pure thought, pure emotion, free-floating particles in a cold universe. Maybe you're just one step closer to that evolutionary state. Ahead of the curve. Sentience, freed from these prisons we call bodies…"

"You're starting to convince me."

She smiled. Lady Gaga faded to Billie Eilish, and the pizza guy whistled another night away.

*

We ended up going back to my apartment on East Broadway and made love until the early hours. When it was over, we sat on my bed and ate some sour cream and onion potato chips that I had lying around— Lay's, of course. Then we opened my window and climbed outside onto my fire escape, sitting there, overlooking the predawn. She put her ear to my chest and listened for an absent heartbeat. Satisfied that there was none to be heard, she leaned her head on my shoulder and took my hand in hers.

I cradled it in my palms and ran my fingertips over the spot where the thumb should have been. If an alien with no knowledge of human anatomy saw this hand, it would never conclude that hers was defective. I told her this, and she laughed softly.

"That's because I have a metaphysical thumb. Like you and your heart— we're not missing anything, really. We're moving closer to that state of pure thought."

"I can't wait to get there."

"Are you happy?"

"I am right now."

"Me too."

We held each other, and the sky started to turn blue.

*

In the morning, she was gone. There was a handwritten note on my kitchen table. Groggy and parched, I poured myself a glass of water from the sink and read the note.

Gone for a while. Had an amazing night last night. Hope to see you sometime.

She had drawn a small heart at the bottom of the note, with an arrow pointing to it beside the words 'your heart'. Aside from this, there was no phone number or address, or any lifeline back to her. I didn't even know her family name. I tried to find her on social media, without success. I spent that morning in a state of lukewarm giddiness, assuming that she'd get in touch sometime soon. Days stretched out into weeks, and weeks became months. I went back to the movie theater almost weekly, hoping to bump into her. But she didn't show.

I kept checking my mailbox for a playful letter, or even a grim one. Any cryptic note would do, but there were none forthcoming.

A handful of winters passed in a blink, and political insurrection mangled the slapdash soul of a nation.

I don't know what happened to the girl. These days, I spend my time reading and figuring out what to have for dinner. I work just enough to get by, bouncing from one unimpressive job to the next. My latest is a stint at the suicide prevention hotline, where I take calls from people with lives even more aimless than mine and try to talk them out of rash decisions. My heart is still missing, but I'm alive, somehow. I occasionally get emails from people trying to interview me about my medical condition, but I delete all of them. I don't need publicity, or a clinical diagnosis. *Where the conceit of reality ends, truth gushes forth from the wild gullies of dreams.* It's a long winter ahead for all of us, and even without a pulse, I feel that I could use the touch of a four-fingered hand over my chest, where my heart should be.

2007

"One of those rare, fleeting moments when everything is perfect."

1. Two of Hearts
2. Cleveland Place
3. Red Plastic Bag
4. East Broadway Rooftops
5. Religion of Love
6. Limousine

1. TWO OF HEARTS

Those cards aren't yours. You stole them.
Nah, they're mine.
But you stole them.
So? I do what I want. It's just a fuckin' Duane Reade.
Still.
Why do you care? It's just playing cards.
Show me the mind reading one again.
Fine. Pick a card.
Got one.
Ok now put it back. Make sure I can't see it—
Here... You sure you're not looking?
I'm not looking.
You swear?
Yeah.
Fine. I'm putting the card back now...
Word.
No tricky shit, okay?

— annnnnd now I'm just gonna shuffle up the deck—
You did something there!
Naw, I'm just shuffling! I swear.
Hurry up.
Chill, dawg, chill! Okay here we go— I'm going to find your card. If I just slap the deck like this—
Okay...
— your card should be on top now. 1, 2, 3— boom. Was it the Queen of clubs?
Nope.
Ah shit, really?
You fucked up!
Fuck. Okay well— here, take the deck. Find your card and show it to me then.
Haha, can't believe you fucked it up.
Guess I'm off today...
Um.
What?
It's not here. The card.
It's not there? Whaaat.
Deadass, it's not here!
Okay, hold up. I think I see it... it's the... two of hearts!
[Pulls the two of hearts out of his pocket]
[Laughing] Fuck you! Deadass, how did you do that?
[Laughing] Ancient Chinese secret.
No for real, how the fuck did you do that?
[Hands her the card] Read what's on the back.
[She turns it over. He spits on the sidewalk]
You read it?
Yeah... Well... That's adorable.
Yeah? You like it?
Haha, it's mad cute.
So will you go out with me?

Um. I'm not sure...

Oh.

I'm just not like, ready for a relationship right now... Like...

Aight. It's fine.

But like, I still wanna be friends...

[Lights a contraband cigarette purchased from someone's older brother] Okay.

Are you mad?

Yeah. No. I don't know.

[Passes her the cigarette. She smokes]

Ever thought of swimming to New Jersey from here?

We could go right now.

Haha, how?

We could build a raft and just sail across the Hudson.

Word! I'm so down.

Really?

Yeah.

But you don't want to go out with me?

[...]

Maybe when we're older.

2. CLEVELAND PLACE

```
6:10 PM

> Yo where you at

home <

> U going to the show?
```

Maybe <

> Mad heads gonna be there

Yea? <

whos playing again <

> Consumer Feedback, Anything Orange

> Fiasco too I think

oh word <

> its at the knitting factory

i cud be down <

what time <

> Im meeting some ppl in Chinatown

> dumplings

> dollar dumplings

any girls gunna be there? <

> I think Melissa, mayb Emily

> lol

deadass? <

> yeh

Emily's hot lol <

> lol

idk tho <

feeling mad lazy <

> i feel that

> but we might go bombing after

> if u wanna come thru

o shit <

yeh <

> u should come get dumplings with us

> come on

> come onnnnnn

mayb <

but i might smoke a blunt first <

> dolo?

> *solo

yea <

free crib rite now <

> oh word

> how long your folks gone for

their in the country for the weekend <

> whaaaaaat

> we out

> can i come over????

> smoke a blunt with u

> plzzz

haha yea come over dude <

im chillin <

> word

> hold up this girl is texting me

> i might go by hers first

horny boy <

> lol

who is it <

> u know Maya D?

> she's one year up

oh word <

naw I dont know her <

> we made out last weekend

oh shit! <

u tryna date her? <

> haha idk

> her parents have a dope place tho

> in soho

nice <

> her dads a famous photographer

> he might hire me to be his assistant

that's cool <

*

8:33 PM

> yoooooooo

> whats good son

hey bro <

nuthin much, just chillin <

thought you were coming over ? <

> I wud but the thing it i cant rijkt now

? <

> Sry lol

> buddy ull never guesss where iam

?? <

> Im in Cleveland

> !!!!!!!!!!!

wtf <

what are u talking about <

> Im in cleveland bro, straight up

> so i cant come over

> ;)

im confused <

> he

> hey

> u know how im in cleveland?

no <

> im at CLEVELAND PLACE bitch

> u kknow the street Cleveland place

> near Lafayette

> hahahahahahAhaha

lol r u drunk? <

> billions of blistering barnacles

> ahoy

dude ur definitely drunk <

i smoked the blunt without u <

> ah noooooo

> fuck u man

> fuck youuuuuuuuuu

haha <

i just checked, the shows at 9 <

i think i might go <

> word

> listen ima come thru

> hold up

> i wanna get fucked up tonite

ur already fucked up dude loll <

> son i wanna DANCE

> go hard

dude ur wilin <

                             *

8:45 PM

> i luv you man

love you too dude <

> see you at the knit factoru?

> *factory

yeah dude <

> im flyin in from CLEVELAND

haha <

> see u then amigo

see you <

3. RED PLASTIC BAG

Shhhhh. Hear that?

What?

I think a train's coming.

Nah, that's on the other track.

You sure? I dunno, it sounds pretty close.

There are no trains on this side bro.

You've been here before right?

Word, I come here all the time.

Can you guys shut the fuck up? I need to finish this piece, making me all nervous and shit.

You're *sure* there are no trains here?

Yeah I told you, it's abandoned.

Yo what do you think of this? My letters are mad nice now.

TOY. *[Laughs]*

Shut up, bro. You can't write for shit.

My bad, just fucking with you. *[Takes a picture on a digital camera. The flash momentarily lights up the walls]*

For real, listen to that. I think there's a train on this side.

Yo chillllll. I'm telling you, we're clear.

Nah son, there's definitely a train coming. I'm gonna go look...

Stop being such a pussy, it's fine.

I'll be right back. *[Walks around the bend]*

Aight.

Yo I heard SAMO did this exact tunnel back in the day.

Deadass? You ever seen any SAMO tags around here?

Nah, but Liam said he did. Probably written over by now.

You ever been to Five Pointz?

Yea. It's kinda stupid though. Like, legal graffiti and shit.

Yeah I don't fuck with that. Buncha sellouts.

Word, it's like people get old and they lose their edge man.

That's not gonna happen to us.

Fuck no. *[Outlines the letter "T" on the wall]* I'm almost done.

Looks nice, dude. *[Snaps another photo]*

Yo hold up, hold up— get one with me in it.

Haha, you got it.

Ok, NOW. *[Holds a can of spray paint in one hand, flips off the camera with the other]*

Beautiful. *[Takes multiple photos. The flash bounces off the walls like a strobe light]*

Put that shit on Flickr.

Haha.

[The sound of footsteps running toward them]

Yo!

What?

There's a fuckin train coming.

What—

I knew it. I saw it, it's coming now.

No way—

For real?

You said there were no trains here, asshole—

What the fuck— I've never seen a train here before—

Fuck this.

We gotta run.

I know, I know. Fuck. Okay.

What are we gonna do?

Hold up, lemme finish this fill-in.

Fuck it, come on let's go.

Chill b! One second.

I'm out.

Where can we go?

The catwalk. There's an emergency hatch over there, by the Bowery.

Dude, I hear it. We gotta run.

Almost done...

Fuck outta here man, drop the fucking paint!

We OUT—

One second—

There's no time—

Let's book it— now, NOW!

A can of spray paint drops to the ground but makes no sound, its echo overpowered by the rush of a Brooklyn-bound Q train. The kids run for their lives, scuffing their sneakers with soot. One of them steps in a shit-filled puddle. Up ahead, there's an old Chinese man with a red plastic bag in hand, standing on the train tracks; he's a hunched silhouette, backlit by the abandoned station in the distance. They freeze, but there's no time: the Q shows no signs of slowing. They scream at the old man: get the fuck outta here! One of them grabs him by the shoulders and tries shoving him along, but he won't budge. The train is bearing down on them; the kids keep running. One of them looks over his shoulder; the old man is still there, transfixed by the Q.

The kids reach the abandoned station just in time. The Q screams by and they huddle around the dusty pillars, waiting for it to pass. It does, ripping through the tunnel and vanishing at the other end. When the coast is clear, they run, passing through a rusty gate, up a flight of stairs, and through an unmarked door. They emerge on the street in front of a Citibank. They say nothing, scanning the block for cops and jaywalking across Canal Street, disappearing into the bright lights of Chinatown.

They agree to never speak of that night.

Down below, a red plastic bag floats through the tunnel; airborne, carried by a draft. It spirals upward on a wave of convection, like some synthetic tumbleweed. Its frayed handles resemble broken animal wings.

It carries the weight of dues paid in full, a life spent in jeopardy, hoping for better days.

The mystery Q tears around the bend and is never seen again.

4. EAST BROADWAY ROOFTOPS

"Yo it's cold dude, can we go inside somewhere?"

"Yeah I'm down."

There's a rundown tenement a few feet away, between an herbal pharmacy and a bootleg DVD store. One of the boys pushes the door at random, and it opens. He grins.

"Busted lock."

"Word!"

"Let's go."

"For real?"

"Yeah!"

"Dope."

They go in, and climb six flights of stairs. At the end of a dingy corridor, one more staircase takes them to the fire ladder and then the roof. A metal door is wedged shut, and one of them kicks it open. It gives with little resistance, and they sit under a tangerine sky. The taller one takes out a bottle.

"Racked this from Gristedes. Love those guys."

"I'm sure they love you too. 'Our most loyal shoplifter.'"

"Haha, fuck you dude. All you've ever done is steal decks of playing cards. I mean what the fuck is that?"

"I'm a magician, so it's not stealing bro. I just make them disappear, and then reappear in my pocket."

"This guy, man. This guy's too much."

They drink, passing the bottle back and forth. It's a forty ounce— known colloquially as piss.

"You know what happened the other day?"

"What."

"I was out with some heads, my mom told me to be home by eleven. Whatever, I stayed at Joey's until pretty late and when I got back my dad was fuckin' wilin' on me man. He shoved me and yelling all like 'who the fuck you think you are, you little shit? You and all your fucking friends— get out of here. Go on. GO. You don't come home at four in the morning, your mom's been calling you all fucking night. You have no respect, you know that?' Then he threw me out."

"Shit man. So what did you do?"

"I went back to Joey's and crashed there. Pretty stupid. His parents were gone for the weekend though so it was fine."

The older boy lights a cigarette. A few rooftops away, someone's throwing a college party.

"That sounds pretty fucked up. My parents are pretty chill; we don't fight that much."

"You're lucky. Or maybe you're doing it wrong. Being a good student and shit."

"Haha."

A rat runs across the rooftop, scampering down a broken ventilation funnel.

"The fucked up thing is, my dad's not a good person."

"Really? He's alright."

"Nah dude. There's some really messed up shit I haven't told you about."

"Oh word?"

"Yeah."

In the distance, the Twin Towers are no longer there. Were they ever?

"My dad's cheating on my mom. Like, multiple times. The guy is a piece of shit."

"Whaaat, for real? How do you know?"

"So my dad goes to Spain every year for work. Last summer, I went with him to help out. And like I didn't know this, but he has this assistant he goes with— some woman from there. We met up there and like I didn't even see him that much. He was working all the time and just left me alone.

His assistant was like showing me around and everything— I think he wanted her to keep tabs on me. He doesn't trust me anymore. She was cool, actually. We just chilled in the apartment together, like watching TV and walking around the city while my dad was working. She's old, like thirty or something. And when my dad got back we'd go have dinner somewhere. It was pretty chill.

One time we were just hanging out in my room and she got on the bed with me. We got all cuddly and stuff. It was really weird, but like I didn't say no. And then all of a sudden we're making out, she takes her shirt off and starts pulling my pants down. I didn't notice before but she was like, really hot. She had really big tits and I'd never been with someone older, you know? We were naked and she tied a shirt around my head, like a blindfold so I couldn't see. She was like you can't look, just let me do it. So I just lay there. Fuck, it was so hot... I still jack off thinking about that."

He pauses for a nicotine intermission. A million lights in Chinatown tonight.

"Then, the next night I go to her room. And what do I see? She's with my dad. They're fucking. I see it cuz the door isn't even completely closed, but they don't see me. They were sleeping together that whole time, man. I'll bet they were doing it every year— every time my dad was in Spain."

"That's heavy, dude. I'm sorry."

"All good."

"Does your mom know about this?"

"I don't think she knows."

"And that woman? Did you guys—?"

"Nah. It was just once."

"Huh."

"But I still think about it."

Pause.

"You ever get head before?"

"Yeah!"

"Oh yeah? Who from?"

"Oh I dunno, just some girl."

"Uh huh. Right."

He smokes.

"When was the last time you hooked up with a girl?"

"Not gonna lie, it's been a while."

"You horny right now?"

"Haha, yeah I'd be down to get with someone."

The first boy has a strange look in his eyes.

"Would you be— this is gonna sound weird—"

"Yeah? What?"

"Wanna make out?"

The second boy laughs and punches his friend on the shoulder.

"What does *that* mean, you going gay on me?"

"Nah dude, I'm just saying— what if like— we could make out and just close our eyes and pretend that we're with girls right now. You feel me?"

Nervous laughter.

"Whoa dude. I don't know, this is weird..."

"Yo come on man, it's nothing. It's not gay or anything. We'll keep our eyes closed and pretend we're kissing girls. It'll feel more real that way, you know?"

The taller boy passes his friend the cigarette. It's almost through.

"Don't you ever get tired of jerking off?"

"Yeah, for sure. But—"

"It just feels so good to touch an actual body, know what I'm saying? Come on, it's not real— we're not fags, I know you like pussy. And you know I'm all about it."

They both laugh, flipping their long hair out of their faces. Then, they kiss.

When it's over, they smoke and watch the skyline slowly lighting up. Neither speaks for some time.

"Wanna go ride the back of a train?"

"Yeah sure."

The taller boy puts out his cigarette. They sit up, get up, and leave the roof; through peeling hallways, past a shriveled auntie just back from a grocery haul, down the stairs onto East Broadway. They stop for dollar dumplings, pay in cash and walk to the Canal Street station. A bored kiosk attendant dozes on the job, and the boys sneak through the turn styles unnoticed. Friday night clubbers crowd out the platform, checking their hair and nails. The train finally arrives ten minutes late, the Halloween whores and balding frat brothers piling into a compartment smelling of cheap liquor and bums. When it leaves the station, the two kids are nowhere to be found.

Then again, a closer look and they might be observed hanging on the back of a Q train crossing the Manhattan Bridge, yelling above the din.

5. RELIGION OF LOVE

If there is to be any religion at all, let it be a religion of love. Free of dogma, it casts a sardonic eye upon other faiths, with humor, curious to hear what they have to say; never brittle and always evolving. The religion of love does not punish except to remind us of our own fallibility. It is not annotated, or enshrined in gospel, but rather, it is felt in our hearts. Love in theory may be pure, but the practice of loving is fraught with beautiful contradiction; purity on earth is a dangerous conceit, and a corollary to evil. If we love truly, there can be no killing, no enslavement, no rape, no torture. There is no god; only love. That is the one true religion.

6. LIMOUSINE

It was one of those filthy Friday nights.

We'd just come from the McDonald's on Chambers Street— and before that, a show at the Knitting Factory. We were sweaty and rude, loose on the streets and looking for our next fix. That's when he drove by in his black limousine.

"Yo!"

One of the girls— a grungy sophomore named Sasha— knocked on the passenger-side window and pressed her nose against the glass. It rolled down, and the driver leaned over to get a better look at us.

"Hey! You busy right now?"

"Just waiting for my guy. I have to pick him up here and drive him home."

He pointed at the club behind us; a VIP pleasure zone called the Red Room. Then, he said:

"But you know what, I'm early. You kids want a ride?"

We couldn't believe our luck.

"Fuck yeah."

There were four of us: two girls and two boys. We piled into the back seat and slammed the door.

"Where to?"

He drove us up to Times Square, right into the obscene heart of it all. One of my friends pulled a bottle of vodka from her orange Jansport backpack and passed it around. Up front, the driver smiled into the rearview mirror and put on some tunes.

We'll walk around
Pretending we're all grown up

Hey, rich girls!
Well, can you tell me why-y-y
You're so stuck up
And act so down?

"Dope! Who's playing?"

"My man, this is *The Virgins*. My favorite band right here."

"Sick."

"Love this song."

Sasha gripped the bottle of vodka around the neck and swayed in time to the music with her eyes closed. She'd smoked a blunt a couple hours before.

"Yo watch out, you're gonna wreck his limo."

"Sorrryyyy."

She passed the bottle to me, and I took a light but convincing swig. The alcohol tasted like a dead end. I looked out the tinted windows and took it all in: the billboards, the tourists, and overpriced hotdog stands; that dreadful butt of all jokes. To love Times Square was to be a philistine; yet in this moment, I privately reveled in its tawdry glow.

"Let's go uptown!"

"Nah, uptown is *lame*. There's nothing going on over there."

"Don't talk shit about uptown."

"Uptown *sucks*. L.E.S. represent!"

"Fuck you, Jack."

Jack and Sasha had an ambiguous kind of fling going—a blueprint for the years of messy entanglements to come.

We *did* end up going uptown, by way of the Westside Highway. This gave our driver a chance to show off his skills at the wheel— cutting across lanes and ripping ahead at twice the speed limit, clearly enjoying himself, ignoring the chorus of angry honking from the commuters and truckers forced to share the road with us. We rolled around in the back, shrieking with laughter, falling onto one another as the limo swerved from side to side. At one point, my phone buzzed. I dug it out of my pocket and flipped it open to a message from my mother. *Where are you*, it said. Before I could reply, the battery suddenly died. This didn't bother me much.

I caught only partial glimpses of the driver's face. He was older than us, but not by much; he could have been someone's elder half brother. He was wearing a chauffeur's cap and a neatly-pressed suit. His complexion was dark, but only just; a vague guess would place him as Latin or Persian— though for the most part this was baseless speculation.

"So where you from, Mr. Driver?"

"I'm from Queens, baby, Jackson Heights."

"My uncle lives in Jackson Heights!"

"One of my buddies used to live in Tribeca, his family moved out to Jackson Heights."

"You kids from Manhattan?"

"Word up!"

"L.E.S!"

The driver registered this information without comment. Only then did it occur to me that maybe, just maybe, this ride wasn't going to be free. Would we end up bound and gagged in some New Jersey warehouse, our parents forced to cough up impossibly large sums of cash to negotiate our safe return? The thought crossed my mind, but was just as quickly banished. Why spoil a perfect night?

After a harrowing detour through the Bronx— harrowing only because we had seldom ventured that far north— he drove us down across the bridge through Harlem and the Upper East Side, past the Friday nighters renting their first trust fund apartments south of 96th street, turning up the volume on whatever perfect song he fancied ("Wow, are you a DJ too?"), never making a single rough stop or poorly-executed turn; this was, clearly, no ordinary driver. As we passed the Empire State building, he explained:

"I've always wanted to be a race car driver, actually. I've loved NASCAR since I was a little kid."

"Woooooow. That's sick."

"You done any races?"

"Oh you know, here and there. Truth is, driving in the city is the best practice you can get. People here can't drive to save their lives. Y'all have your licenses?"

"Nope."

"No way."

"What's the point? We just take the train."

I could see the driver shaking his head in the rearview mirror.

"That's the problem with you kids. You think you'll live in the city your whole lives, never have to learn how to drive. Someone else will always get you where you need to be, right? Cab drivers, train conductors, whatever. But sooner or later, y'all will have to learn. Trust me on that."

He laughed. We were only half-listening, tuning out these inconvenient truths. Personally, I had a special talent back then— a talent for filtering out useful information and keeping only the trivial bits. We all did. Bunch of prodigies right here; the leaders of tomorrow. Tomorrow, it turns out, isn't all it's cracked up to be. It zips right by with no warning, and by the time you see it on your calendar, it's already past. Maybe one of us— the "leaders of tomorrow"—

will solve this problem. So far, the adults don't seem to have made much progress. If they had, they'd all be a lot younger.

"I got my start driving cabs— normal taxis, right— years back, and doing illegal street racing after work out in Queens. Used to go crazy in Willets Point, late at night when all the auto shops were closed. Crashed my car into a junk pile once— actually, it was my dad's car. Should've seen him when he found out. But in my opinion, I did him a favor. That car wasn't worth shit, you know? It was all beat up, didn't drive right. About time he got another car anyway. He didn't appreciate it though— not then, not now."

We plowed down Broadway, edging an obnoxious red Ferrari into the neighboring lane. The car's owner revved his engine in a bid to intimidate. Our driver took no notice.

"Anyway. The race car thing hasn't worked out just yet, but I do okay. Main thing is that I'm still driving— as long as I'm driving, I've got no complaints."

None of us knew what to say to this, so we just sat in the back and nodded drunkenly. Someone had their hand around my shoulder— it could have been any of them, though I can't remember who. I recall feeling vaguely horny. We spent the last minutes of our ride in boozy contentment until he dropped us off back downtown.

"Yo thanks so much brother."

"That was awesome, thank you!"

"Soooooo dope!"

The driver nodded and started to roll up the window.

"Y'all take care, okay? Don't get in trouble."

As we set off toward the end of the block, I spotted a man leaving the Red Room; some asshole, probably a former member of an Ivy League frat house. Our driver came out, opened the passenger door for him, and shut it before getting back behind the wheel and driving away. I thought no more about it and clomped off down the street with my friends, tired but restless, aching for another round of thrills.

*

Many years later.

It's a countdown to midnight. Everyone's out, taking advantage of the unseasonably warm December evening; the Christmas spillover is running its raucous way through every corner of the city, ushering in the new year with apocalypse and wine.

Times Square is swarming with the usual suspects. Tonight, I'm right in the thick of it, snooping around incognito, burning away the final moments of the year with an uncertain heart and falafel in hand. Aside from a few grim looking cops, everyone's out to party; but me, I'm alone.

For me, this is more than simply the turning of the collective clock. This is the one night where I shed my protective skin, slide into a pair of old jeans and head for the spectacle, just as much a tourist as anyone else. Sometimes, I even wear a baseball cap.

Ten minutes to go.

I'm walking along 42nd Street, past the theaters and roasted nut vendors. I don't live here, I tell myself, whimsically. I'm visiting from Kentucky, or Barcelona.

Just then, a car pulls up to the curb and the side door opens; a pair of heels hits the pavement beside me, followed by legs, followed by a gang of overdressed college girls.

They loiter on the sidewalk in identical Kim Kardashian outfits, blocking my path, staring into their phones. Momentarily forgetting that I'm undercover, I begin to snarl in their general direction— cursing their suburban childhoods, mocking their candy cane perfume— until I notice the car that dropped them here. In particular, the driver.

It's him.

He's older, we're all older. He's standing by the side of the car, taking a smoke break. It's a different limousine— longer than the one I remembered— but still a limousine. I decide to hang around.

"Happy New Year," I say.

He looks my way and raises his cigarette in acknowledgement.

"Not yet, my man. Still got a few minutes."

I nod.

"Fair enough."

I'm expecting something— at least a flicker of recognition. But he appears not to remember.

Out of nowhere, he turns to me:

"Want a ride?"

This is exactly what I wanted to hear.

"I mean, sure. If you're not busy. You don't have to wait for those girls? I mean, those fine young women?"

He chuckles faintly between puffs before flicking his cigarette onto the sidewalk.

"Come on, get in."

"You sure?"

"Absolutely. It's on me."

I thank him and start to open the door to the back seat, but he stops me.

"Get in the front with me my man."

"Really?"

Then I'm in the front seat, and we're off. As far as I can tell, there's no destination; in any case, I don't much care where we go. There's a song playing, one I don't recognize. It's good, though.

He doesn't remember me yet— after all, he's driven thousands if not millions of passengers at this point. I want to say something, but for some reason, I hold back. For the moment, I'm content to just sit and enjoy the ride.

"You got anyone to share New Year's with?"

The driver shakes his head to the beat.

"If you're talking wife, husband, kids, or part-time lovers, then nope. I guess I'll be spending the last few minutes of this year with *you*."

There's a bitter edge in his voice I hadn't noticed the first time. Something's hanging onto the ends of his words, a kind of resignation. All the same, I'm happy to be here.

"I don't have anyone either, to be honest. Spending the countdown with you? I'll take it."

He waves away my small talk and drifts into the next lane. Even his driving is different, I think to myself. He's still in command, but it feels heavy, somehow. I clear my throat.

"You been driving a long time?"

"Ohhh yeah. Long time."

"You know, I'm not really the kind of guy to ride in limos. But this is the second time for me."

I want him to ask me about the first time, but he simply nods and keeps driving.

"Um, anyway, you from the City?"

"Jackson Heights, Queens. Still there, probably gonna life it at this point. Gotta take care of my mother, you know?"

We take a left turn and head across town.

"Do you give free rides like this a lot?"

"Naw, not that much. Too many crazies out there. And it wouldn't look too good for the company if I got caught."

"Hey, you should watch out— I might be one of those crazies."

He shakes his head.

"No, I can tell. You're alright."

"Glad to be here, man."

We take a right and head down 2nd Avenue. Then, he says:

"First time I ever picked anyone up was years ago. It was a bunch of kids. They were certainly crazy, but they were real cool too. I dunno, they kind of reminded me of myself, from back in the day."

I give him a knowing look, but he's staring straight ahead.

"Back then, I wanted to be a race car driver. Can you imagine? Gotta be some kinda crazy to do that."

"So what happened? You're not about it anymore? NASCAR?"

"Nah man. But this job's alright. Been doing it a long time. If I'm driving, I'm happy. No complaints here."

"That's good. It's not too late though, is it? You could still get in the game."

He shakes his head again and smiles a far-off smile. I suddenly feel very young and foolish.

Two minutes to midnight. I report this live update to the driver, who takes it without comment. A couple of jocks point and wave as they cross the street in front of us.

"This year is gonna be a strange one. I can feel it."

"What makes you say that?"

"There are signs everywhere, my man.

"What kind of signs?"

He just shakes his head.

"I'd better get back to 42nd— those girls will be waiting for their driver."

"No worries. Do what you gotta do."

We circle back around to Times Square. One minute to go.

He lets me off at the same spot, in front of a McDonald's. The year has entered its denouement and the crowd is counting down in feverish, clumsy unison.

5...

4...

Three..

Two...

ONE...

The driver turns to me.

"Happy New Year, my guy."

"Happy New Year. And thanks for the ride."

We shake hands, and I try giving him a tip.

"Thank you sir, but not tonight. I'm just glad I got to spend New Year's Eve with someone, you feel me?"

"Likewise. Still, I want you to take it..."

"Nope, nope."

Finally, I relent. We shake hands again and I bid the driver good night. I'm on the verge of confessing— telling him that I was one of those "kids" he picked up back in 2007. But then again, if he didn't recognize me now, there seemed little point. Some memories, it seems, should be left alone. I open the car door and leave. Times Square is apoplectic with joy, a carnival of screams and confetti. What are we celebrating, exactly? Try as I might to understand, I'm not completely sure. A free-falling beer bottle sails through the air and smashes on the sidewalk a few feet away.

Another year goes out with a bang.

*

They find the limo a few months later, wrecked to pieces.

A headline in the *New York Post* declares the "JOYRIDE TO HELL" a street race gone awry. The writer goes on to explain: an employee at a luxury car service stole one of the company limousines and drove it out to deep Queens in the dead of night. Eyewitnesses confirm several sightings of the limousine and another car driving through quiet residential streets at breakneck speeds, skidding around corners and running through red lights.

I stare at his picture— a grainy image pulled from the internet. He's wearing a baseball cap and headphones, smiling for a photo he clearly took himself. Without his uniform, he looks distressingly ordinary; but it's him, just the same.

When authorities recovered the two vehicles, there was no sign of him; the other driver was found dead in his car. Preliminary reports neither confirm nor deny the death of the limousine driver; pending the results of the ongoing investigation, "all we can do is speculate at this point." There are mentions of debt and wagers, but nothing is certain. "At this time, the driver of the limousine is being treated as both a victim and a perpetrator— at minimum, an accessory to manslaughter."

Both a victim and a perpetrator. Doesn't this describe pretty much everyone, I wonder out loud.

*

I'm not sure what role— if any— I played in the driver's final act. For that matter, I can't be sure that it *was*, in fact, his farewell; they never found his body. There are days where I replay that New Year's Eve over and over, lingering on our admittedly stiff and subdued conversation, mining my memory for clues. Something I said to him near the end of our ride continues to haunt me:

It's not too late though, is it?

Maybe I, in a moment of blithe presumption, planted the seed of bad ideas; a false hope that would grow in his mind like a cancer, seeping into the desiccated grooves carved out by loss and regret, promising to turn back the new year in contempt of time. Would he still be here, if not for my trite opinions?

On the other hand, maybe the crash was deliberate. More likely, the crash itself was an accident, but perhaps entering that race was a decision he owned; a reset, an act of agency. Maybe he was prepared to burn out, rather than wither away.

Whatever the case may be, I salute him.

It's really not my place to say. But he's still missing, not yet officially dead; and I hope against hope that he's out there somewhere, cruising down a technicolor highway, the specter of mortality trailing in hot pursuit— determined to catch this misty-eyed fugitive; but he's one step ahead, calmly pressing the accelerator while he cranks up the volume on some underground radio hit; he is driver and passenger, owing nothing to no one, so terribly free.

SHANGHAI SYLVIA

I knew Mei from the old days. It was a short, puzzling two months of my life that I haven't thought about much—but that I find myself revisiting as of late. I was studying at the Curtis Institute of Music in Philadelphia at the time, living with three other musicians in a crooked house over in Fishtown. When one of our roommates moved out, we posted an advertisement online for the vacant room. Mei was the only person who answered the ad. We would have preferred another musician, but we couldn't afford to be picky. Within a week, Mei had moved in and taken over the fourth room.

Mei didn't say much, and we knew very little about her. Getting her to talk was like going fishing in a lake with no fish. As far as we could tell, she wasn't a student, and didn't appear to have a job. We, on the other hand, practiced our instruments constantly. The house was a menagerie of sound, from midnight preludes to early morning sonatas. We warned Mei about our routine before she moved in, but she insisted that it would not be a problem. In fact, she was something of a music connoisseur. During her stay, she would periodically barge into our rooms unannounced just to sit there and watch us while we played our scales. It was unnerving, but we never turned down an opportunity to play for someone without musical training. When we asked for her feedback, her comments were surprisingly insightful. I'd even say that her critiques were far more helpful than the pedantic ravings of my professors at school. My other roommates agreed. Every night, we'd gather in the living room and play through our repertoire for Mei. After each performance, she'd deliver a blunt assessment of our work, picking apart the technically flawless yet ultimately failed renderings of Debussy and Saariaho with an erudition that far outshone our own feeble attempts at artistry. For someone without any musical pedigree, she was more musical than any of us. Mei should have been a musician—or at the very least, a music critic. When I told her this, she pretended not to hear me.

After she left, our creaky salon felt oddly bereft. We ended up finding a friendly tuba player to take her place, but a pall hung over the house. Our practice sessions felt listless and hollow, as if we were playing melodies through a telephone with nobody at the other end of the line. A few months later, I decided to move in with my girlfriend on the other side of town, leaving that house forever.

Half a lifetime has passed since then. I'm married now, living out a comfortable and mildly underwhelming existence in Jackson Heights, Queens. My wife is a literature professor at NYU, and I've lucked into a steady career at a cybersecurity firm in midtown. My musician days are long gone.

A few weeks ago, I received a message from Mei. We hadn't spoken in over twenty years, and I couldn't believe she even remembered who I was. When I saw her note, my curiosity spiked to levels unseen since college. She had absolutely no reason to write to me. We were not friends, old lovers, or even colleagues. Part of me hoped that she was in town; maybe she would ask me to have coffee. But she extended no such invitation. Without any preamble, she launched into a lengthy account of a strange night from many years ago— an incredible story that defied the limitations of the physical universe. Her retelling was so thorough, so vivid, that I found myself believing it over the objections of my hard-earned common sense.

It all started at a mail recovery center in Atlanta, Georgia.

*

All kinds of things end up at the Mail Recovery Center — previously known as the Dead Letter Office, and the Ministry of Dead Letters before that— a flat, unassuming brick building on the outskirts of Atlanta. Despite the best efforts of the Postal Service, some mail is simply undeliverable. Once condemned, these "dead letters" are sent to the processing facility where their fate is reassigned by a team of unionized mail specialists. Unclaimed packages, misspelt addresses— many roads lead to the Ministry. Simple letters lacking monetary value are usually tossed out, while larger objects are occasionally put up for auction. Stray cash is seized by the Postal Service, or pocketed by an unscrupulous mail handler. Suspicious arrivals— unidentified powders, dubious unmarked pills— are turned over to the police. About 20,000 pieces of "dead mail" enter the Ministry every single day. Very few make it back out.

Mei was a low-level worker there, and something of an enigma. Mei wasn't from Atlanta. In fact, she wasn't even from Georgia. A native of Sunset Park, Brooklyn, she fled the stifling pretensions of New York City years ago and somehow ended up in Atlanta after a series of hellish Greyhound bus rides. As a teenager, she spent her weekends running wild and recreating, scene by scene, the drug-soaked exploits of the kids from *Kids* (a 1995 cult film about delinquent city youth). Her parents, nonplussed by their wayward offspring, tried in vain to correct course. But their constant nagging only incited her to further misconduct, causing their relationship to sour into silence. A single, tedious semester of collegiate studies at Hunter College proved to be an embarrassing dud, and she quietly dropped out after failing to attend her final exams.

By this time, Mei was a confirmed castout from the mainstream.

Unsure of where to go, she took refuge with a few bohemians in an industrial warehouse in Bushwick, Brooklyn. When she had tired of the parties and the bad art, she took a bus to Philadelphia and fell in with an eccentric gang of classical musicians living in a communal house. Being in a new city afforded a certain novelty, and she enjoyed waking up to the melodious sounds of cellos and trumpets. But this was short-lived. Mei ended up hitching a ride to Baltimore a couple months later, and then to Washington D.C., following some vague, tacit directive that pulled her ever-southward. During this time, she supported herself through a combination of waitressing, food delivery, and teaching English over the internet. When funds were low, she briefly took up dancing in a roadside strip club near Savannah. Her stage name was "Shanghai Sylvia".

Despite her unconventional resumé, Mei somehow landed a job at the Ministry of Dead Letters. The decision to hire her was most likely made *in erratum*— an administrative hiccup, a casualty of American exceptionalism.

Mei didn't talk much to her colleagues, unless it was about mail. At the end of the work day, she would leave the premises with barely a nod and disappear into the sprawl. Unlike most residents, she did not own a car; an unthinkable privation around these parts. Instead, to the bewilderment of her colleagues, Mei preferred to walk and brave the halfhearted patchwork of trams and buses that passed for public transportation down South. Admitting this to the locals was tantamount to a kind of treason— akin to a declaration of vegetarianism in front of a steakhouse, or a conscientious abstention from alcohol during a hazing ritual. Accordingly, their reactions generally ranged from defensive to grudging, to outright hostile. This didn't bother Mei, though. Half the time she couldn't even understand what they were saying through their accents.

This night was no different from any other. Everyone else had gone home, but Mei was still at her desk, working overtime. She was not actually required to be here at this hour, but Mei enjoyed the sepulchral calm of the office— with its featureless grid of cubicles from the 1990s and the rows of abrasive overhead lights. Taking advantage of the empty space, Mei had her phone plugged into a pair of speakers that she'd brought from her apartment, playing

DJ to celebrate another night of solitude. Tonight's featured tune: Bach's fifth keyboard concerto in F minor, performed by Glenn Gould. As far as Mei was concerned, Glenn Gould was the only pianist worth a damn. As a fellow iconoclast, she felt a kinship with him that few others could ever hope to understand. Whenever he tickled the ivories, her heart stirred in kind.

While other young people lapped up the confectionary pop that clogged the airwaves— among other genres of the day— Mei studiously avoided these and instead filled her ears with all manner of musical esoterica. In the catalogue of her mind, sixteenth-century madrigals rubbed shoulders with obscure rappers from Brooklyn who would never see fame. Some might call this snobbery. She would not disagree with them.

It was nearly midnight, but Mei had no plans to head home just yet. Humming along to Glenn Gould's irascible rendition of the fifth concerto, she sifted through a large stack of mail, unsealing envelopes and checking their contents for valuable goods before throwing them away. Tonight, the piles were full of misplaced family heirlooms, lost in transit and now condemned to a lonely death by auction or the garbage compactor. The Ministry would occasionally indulge tough cases and try to track down the senders, but such altruism was generally beyond the organization's budget.

When she'd finished sorting her batch of mail, Mei got up from her chair and left the cubicle, walking down a long corridor to the central mail depot. This was the dumping ground for "dead letters"— the unsorted collection of strays. The walls were lined with oversized baskets of letters and teetering stacks of cardboard boxes. Mei turned on the lights and grabbed an empty mail bin from a stack in the corner. Then, she froze. There was someone else in the room.

A very short man— at least, something that looked like a man— was rummaging through a letter basket. He was obscenely short; there was no way he cleared three feet. But he wasn't just short, he was *small*. Like a child. He was wearing shorts and high socks, and carrying a sack over his shoulder. Like Santa Claus. The man turned around and smiled at Mei. His face was old and wrinkled, with a frizzy white beard and a gigantic nose. He didn't seem the slightest bit perturbed by her entry.

"Howdy!"

The short man cleared his throat.

"Hope I didn't startle you. I thought everyone had gone home."

Mei gulped and squeezed the mail bin.

"Um, they have."

"Ah, but *you're* still here. That's good, very good."

"You have to leave, now."

"No, no, I can't. I just need a little more time— please! My haul has been pretty lackluster tonight. Just let me scrounge around for a few more minutes, and then I'll be out of your hair."

"What are you doing?"

"I'm uh, well the thing is, I'm a mail gremlin."

"A *mail gremlin?*"

"Yes, ma'am. That is, I'm a kind of collector. My specialty is 'dead letters', as you call them. You know, the stuff that nobody wants. 'Give me your sick, give me your poor', and all that."

"You're not allowed in here."

"Well now, you could say that I have a kind of... informal arrangement with the head honchos around here..."

"I doubt that."

The mail gremlin took out a handkerchief and blew his nose, which was beet red. He looked like one of the seven dwarves in Snow White.

"Say, have we met before? You look awfully familiar."

"No. I think I'd remember someone like you."

"Oh, really now? You think I look funny?"

"Yes."

The mail gremlin cackled uproariously. Then he stowed his handkerchief and took out a can of beer from his coat pocket, cracked it open, and took a swig. Mei started backing toward the doorway. The mail gremlin gave her a sideways look between gulps of beer.

"Look, I'll be out of here soon. No need to call in the cavalry. I'm just a simple mail gremlin, nothing more. I mean, come on. Do I look dangerous to you? I'm three feet tall, a sad old drunk."

Mei stared doubtfully at the mail gremlin. He looked somewhat ragged, but not especially threatening. The sack over his shoulder— a battered, military green scrap of fabric — was, indeed, comical. The mail gremlin drained his beer and pocketed the can, leaning contentedly against a stack of cardboard boxes. Then he took out another can of beer and extended it in Mei's direction.

"Join me?"

Rolling her eyes, Mei propped the mail bin against the wall and cautiously approached the mail gremlin. One of his eyelids drooped, and he looked half asleep. She sat down on the floor opposite him and accepted his offering, guardedly.

"Thanks."

"My pleasure, my pleasure!"

Mei took a sip of beer. Not the worst beer she'd ever had, but not especially good either.

"This isn't the worst beer I've ever had, but it's not especially good either."

The mail gremlin chuckled, and blew his nose.

"Well said, well said!"

Mei examined the can. A Brooklyn brand.

"This beer isn't from around here, is it?"

"Nope. You see, I'm not from around here, either."

"Oh yeah?"

"No way, I'm no Southerner. I'm from New York."

"Oh."

Mei took another sip of beer.

"Come to think of it, you don't sound like a local either. Not that that means much anyway— these days, everyone's all mixed up, everyone kinda sounds the same. But you're *not* from around here, are you?"

"No, I'm not. Actually, I'm from New York, too."

"Really now! Why didn't you *say* so? Jesus. Which neighborhood?"

"Sunset Park."

"*Sunset Park?* This is fantastic. I'm from Bay Ridge, myself. What a small world!"

"Tiny."

"Let's drink to that."

He produced another can of beer from his jacket pocket — which seemed strangely bottomless— opened it, and raised it in toast. Mei nodded and lifted her own can. Soon, the scent of alcohol filled the windowless room with a boozy lassitude. The mail gremlin watched her; his expression could be described as paternal, and a bit sleepy.

Mei imagined him as a baby, poking his ugly head out of a public mailbox in Bay Ridge before being unceremoniously shoved out onto the dirty pavement.

"So what are you doing down here? Why did you leave, what was it, *Sunset Park?*"

Mei took a swig of beer and thought it over. The flavor seemed to improve with each sip; earthy, slightly fruity.

"It's hard to explain. But can I ask *you* something?"

"For sure, for sure. Doesn't bother me— I like talking. Ask away!"

"Why are you interested in all this junk? It's just other people's mail."

The mail gremlin picked up a cardboard box and began to inspect it. He examined it from every angle, holding it up and shaking it next to his ear. Then he took out a knife and sliced through the top of the box, running the blade through the protective tape and retrieving the contents of the package with his other hand. It was a baseball cap, emblazoned with a timeless political slogan that was either messianic or obscene, depending on your district. The mail gremlin let out a wheeze of delight and put on the hat.

"How do I look?"

"Like a patriot."

"Yee-haw!"

He started prancing around the storage room, the dirty green sack bouncing over his shoulder.

"The truth is, I collect rejects. Like foraging. The stuff that falls through the cracks, all that unwanted junk— I'll take it off your hands, no questions asked. 'Give me your sick, give me your poor'..."

"That's an interesting hobby."

"Ho ho, but it's *not* a hobby, young lady."

"Why do you do it?"

The mail gremlin set about filling his green sack while Mei watched him with some apprehension. Although there was a surveillance camera in the upper corner near the ceiling, Mei made no effort to stop the mail gremlin from plundering the storage room. When her superiors discovered this outrage— and Mei's complicity— there would be an investigation, reprimand, and possibly termination. Mei took another swig of beer. The mail gremlin was looking her up and down.

"It's strange, but I really do feel like I know you."

"We've never met."

"I guess not. But still..."

The mail gremlin squinted at her. Then, his eyes lit up.

"Hold on a minute... Are you... Shanghai Sylvia?"

Mei gulped. But she made no denial. The mail gremlin squealed and clapped his hands.

"I knew it! I *knew* it! Hot damn, you *are* Shanghai Sylvia! Of course, you look totally different offstage. But, wow, I'll never forget that dancing... Let me tell you, you're a rare talent. I've been to quite a few strip clubs in my day, and I've never seen anything like it."

Mei finished her beer and wiped her mouth. Then she tossed the can on the floor.

"So you were a regular, huh."

"You bet I was. Best damn club around."

"It was a total dump."

"Shanghai Sylvia, in the flesh... Just, wow. I never thought I'd see you again."

"What luck."

The mail gremlin's mouth hung open at a cartoonish angle. With his inflammatory baseball cap, oversized nose, and dirty green sack, he looked like a complete imbecile.

"Look, I know it's not for me to say... but you were a *sensation* up there. Like you were born to dance."

"I don't do that stuff anymore. And anyway, I was only there for two months."

"And what a glorious two months it was!"

"Not really. I'd rather forget them."

The mail gremlin began hopping on one foot and then the other, stretching his legs experimentally. One set of shoelaces came undone, flapping noisily around his ankles. He appeared not to notice.

"Forget them?"

"Yes."

"But you were so *good* at it."

"Sometimes we're good at the things we hate— and bad at the things we love."

"A philosopher, too? Wowwee. I'm smitten."

After a particularly vigorous hop, the mail gremlin tripped on his shoelaces and fell face-forward onto the floor. He picked himself up with a grin, straightened his back, and adjusted the brim of his baseball cap. For an old gremlin, he was pretty spry.

"Can I ask you for something? A favor?"

"Depends on what it is."

"How would you *really* like to forget what happened during those two months?"

"What do you mean?"

"In a manner of speaking, I can take care of that for you. If you really want it, that is."

"What are you talking about?"

The mail gremlin rubbed his hands together. Mei eyed him warily.

"The truth is, I'm starving. Famished. I'm desperate. I can't eat normal food— I just puke it right up. I need something a little more..."

"Yeah?"

The mail gremlin fidgeted uneasily, trying to find the right words.

"If you give me your memories— voluntarily, of course— then I can eat, and you can forget. Do you follow what I'm saying?"

"You eat *memories?*"

"In a manner of speaking."

Mei stared hard at this squat, pitiable creature before her.

"Hold on a minute. So you're saying I give you my memories, and then they're gone? Just like that?"

"You won't remember a thing. And I won't starve. It's a win-win!"

In her mind, Mei replayed the chain of events that landed her in this room. The past few years contained so many regrettable episodes, it was hard to keep track. Each time the playback loop snagged on some bitter recollection, she shuddered. Whether there were, on balance, more precious memories than painful ones, she couldn't say. The truth was, Mei already had difficulty remembering much from the past ten years. When she tried to trace the line from college dropout to mail recovery clerk, all she could see was a blurry montage of garbled disappointments. If she concentrated, she could faintly recall a few voices— some friendly, some not— but there was no cohesion to her reminiscences.

"Does this really work?"

"Absolutely. Got bad memories? I'm on the case. Just dump 'em here, and you'll never hear from them again. Guaranteed."

"And how do I do this, exactly? You can't just *eat* memories."

"Here."

The mail gremlin reached deep into his voluminous pockets and produced a tattered notebook. He flipped it open to a blank page, retrieved a pen from a different pocket, and handed Mei the two items.

"What's this for?"

"Write down everything— anything you can remember. Whatever it is you want gone, just jot it down in this here notebook. But don't leave anything out. The more you tell, the more you forget, see?"

"That's it? I just write it down?"

"Giddy up!"

What the hell, Mei thought to herself, scribbling across the page to release the ink from the pen. After a few strokes, lines of black chicken scratch began to appear.

At first, Mei was at a loss. From the aftermath of affairs gone rancid to the implosion of dear friendships, the list of candidates for erasure seemed endless. But in the end, her mind kept circling back to the same interval: those two months. A psychoactive darkness behind the curtain. She squeezed the pen.

"It wasn't even about the dancing, really."

"Eh? What are you on about?"

Mei didn't realize that she had spoken out loud, at first. The mail gremlin was eyeing her curiously.

"Oh, nothing. Just thinking."

She began to write. Visions, smells— contours of memory that she had worked hard to bury— were painfully exhumed and laid bare. Shanghai Sylvia was splayed open on the page, staring back at Mei with the hollow eyes of a taxidermic animal. The mail gremlin watched her, fiddling with his baseball cap. When she was finished, Mei asked the mail gremlin for another can of beer.

"Why certainly, certainly!"

From the recesses of his coat, he whipped out another can which Mei accepted with a curt nod.

"Obliged."

She cracked it open and took a long draft. Then she wiped her mouth and handed the mail gremlin the notebook.

"Here it is. I don't know what you plan on doing with that, but it makes no difference to me."

The mail gremlin took out a magnifying glass and examined Mei's composition, which filled the entirety of one page. He let out a low whistle.

"Now *that's* a doozy. I'm sorry to hear about all of that, I really am. I guess even at my age, you could say that I'm pretty naïve. Jeez. Well—"

With a sudden movement, he tore the page out of the notebook and crumpled it up into a ball. Then he popped it in his mouth, gulped it down, and let out a satisfied belch. Mei stared at him incredulously.

"Well, it's done. Thank you for that— quite a memory you fed me. It's bold and sophisticated, with a pleasantly bitter aftertaste. Raw. I feel great now."

He smiled moronically.

"Would you look at that— this turned out to be a great haul, go figure!"

"Cheers."

"And you. How do you feel?"

Mei was starting to feel lightheaded, but she blamed this on the beer. Other than that, nothing.

"The same. I don't feel any different."

"Oh?"

"I guess you don't have any superpowers after all. Besides being able to eat paper."

The mail gremlin chuckled, and looked at his watch.

"Well, I think I'll get going now. It's late. Listen, this has been a very special evening— for me, anyway."

"It's been a pretty crazy night for sure."

The mail gremlin hoisted the dirty green sack over his shoulder and extended his grubby palm. They shook hands.

"Well, *Shanghai Sylvia,* if you ever need anything, I'm your guy. Just ask. My talents are few and far between— one might even say useless— but I've got a good heart, and I'm your number one fan. I wish you all the best. And— I daresay— if you ever decide to return to the stage, I'll be there."

"The stage? Who's Shanghai Sylvia?"

The mail gremlin beamed.

"Good night!"

"Good night."

The mail gremlin turned on his heel and trundled off to the side door at the other end of the storage room, dragging his sack full of loot across the floor. Then he pushed the metal bar and slipped out into the night. The door banged shut behind him, leaving Mei alone in a room full of beer cans, dead letters, and fading memories.

*

After that, the mail gremlin disappeared.

In her message, Mei told me all about their encounter—along with a rather clinical summary of her life after she left Philadelphia. Her account was thoughtful and penetrating; it read like one of her musical critiques. Without a trace of sentiment, she admitted that she was still unable to recall those two months of her life that she'd forfeited to the mail gremlin. Years of "personal investigation" had yielded only piecemeal results: she now remembered, vaguely, the meaning of "Shanghai Sylvia"—but crucial details were still missing, those which had been expunged from the official record. *They've been blacked out*, she said. *I feel like they contain something important, but I don't know what that is. Please be on the lookout for a mail gremlin. That's all I wanted to say*, she concluded, summarily.

I reread her messages twice, stunned by the enormous blocks of text that felt both cryptic and confessional. Afterward, I found myself speculating presumptuously about the contents of those lost memories: two months of her life, gobbled up by a sly, hungry dwarf in a baseball cap. I tried to glean some ulterior meaning from between the lines, but ultimately turned up short. I couldn't tell if she was asking for my help, or simply warning me that there was a mail gremlin on the loose. Either way, I was ill-equipped to help her. No imagination, as Mei would have said. Just like my lackluster musical performances.

Incidentally, the piece of music she'd been listening to that night— Bach's fifth keyboard concerto in F minor—was the same piece I'd been practicing endlessly back in Fishtown, during Mei's brief residency in our house. She must have heard me play it hundreds if not thousands of times. Personally, I didn't think much of Glenn Gould. Why did she include that particular detail in her message?

This seemed significant to me, but Mei did not elaborate. I guess she just liked that piece.

I immediately drafted a response, deleting and rewriting it several times. *That's an unbelievable story*, I eventually blurted out. *Thanks for writing. How are you? The house was never the same after you left. I'm living in Queens, now. Where are you? Aren't you from Brooklyn? Would love to see you. What are you up to? Are you a music critic yet? Are you still in Atlanta?*

She never responded.

*

I'm walking along Roosevelt Boulevard, in the shadow of the elevated subway tracks. The 7 train shakes up the whole street as it rattles overhead, packed full of daydreamers. It rained last night, so the roads are slick and the air is damp. I stop in at my favorite restaurant and order a plate of rice and beans. I wonder if Mei read my reply, or if she even received it. For all I knew, my message never made it to its destination— a piece of dead mail. There must be dead mail, even in cyberspace, I think to myself. For someone working in cybersecurity, this is an intriguing thought. What would that look like? What kinds of messages could possibly elude the Orwellian precision of the digital trail? Is there such a thing as falling through the cracks of cyberspace? These conundrums last me through my plate of rice and beans.

I don't know what possessed Mei to write me that message. We spent only a moment together before becoming footnotes in each other's lives. I suppose it wasn't really intended for me, exactly. She could have written that to anyone. Like a piece of dead mail, sent out into an uncertain sea of letters with the hopes of reaching just one sympathetic eye. With any luck, the mail gremlin just might find your letter and throw it into his sack for posterity. But then, I thought, he might eat your memories. I ponder this imagery for a moment. I wonder if Mei will ever retrieve those two months she lost. I think about her brief appearance in my own life— which lasted, by chance, exactly two months. In a way, that time has been stolen from me, too, locked in a dream.

Whatever Mei was doing during those two months, that's her business. They may contain multitudes, or simply burn quietly. I hope she finds them. If I ever see the mail gremlin, I'll do my best to get him to talk.

My phone buzzes: a grocery list from my wife. Time to get going. I pay at the counter and leave a fat tip, fishing out a few dollar bills from my wallet and dropping them by the register. Then I leave the restaurant and step out into the muggy afternoon sun, feeling full but not quite satiated, looking for something that I may have forgotten, but whose name escapes me.

THE COURIER

When the knocking started, I had been enjoying a pleasantly erotic dream featuring someone who was not my partner. In this particular scene, I played myself and a former classmate played the role of a stranger. Regretfully, I was not reenacting a steamy encounter from our adolescence but instead conjuring hypotheticals. Everything about this person was just as it was when I'd known her in high school: same long red braid, same crooked nose, same low, raspy tenor drawl. Except that in my dream, it wasn't her. This apparition possessed the same qualities and physical trademarks as the real-life subject, but I knew somehow that she was an imposter. It looked like her, but my intuition told me that it was something else entirely.

We were contorted into a breathless position when I was abruptly awakened by three knocks at the door. They were not especially loud or aggressive, but they woke me nonetheless. I sat up, blinked, and stared in the direction of my front door. Beside me, my partner was asleep— her face sinking into an oversized pillow. We don't have curtains in our apartment, so a thin film of moonlight entered through the window. I shook my partner, but she was resolutely out cold. Three knocks, again. A delicate yet firm touch. My partner rolled over, fitfully, onto my pillow. Resigned to another sleepless night and slightly alarmed, I tossed aside my sheets and put on an old t-shirt before creeping cautiously out of my room and up to the front door. I closed one eye and peered nervously through the peephole.

Staring back at me from the other side of the peephole was my partner. The same one who lay sprawled out in bed, sound asleep. And she wasn't just waiting outside my door: she was looking directly into the peephole, her eyes locked on mine through the one-way prism. I glanced back at my bed through the door that I'd left open. She was still there, sound asleep. I looked through the peephole again. There was no question: my partner was standing outside my front door, staring me down.

Except, it wasn't her. Like the girl in my dream, this vision was a carbon copy of someone real— yet I knew, somehow, that it wasn't the same person. Her face was identical in every way to that of the woman lying in my bed, but it was as if her being were composed of an entirely different set of molecules. Somehow, this thing had assumed— or stolen— my partner's form and appeared at my front door. I didn't know what time it was, but based on the grogginess index I'd say around 1 or 2 AM.

"Who is it?"

Silence. Then:

"Delivery for Mr. Chang."

Delivery? At 2 AM?

"What's this all about? Who are you?"

I closed one eye and squinted through the peephole again. She was, in fact, holding a small cardboard box out in front of her with both hands. Not only that, but she was wearing what looked like an official courier's uniform: khaki shirt with the sleeves rolled up, tucked into a pair of matching shorts. Her deep black hair was pulled back in a tight ponytail. My partner never wore ponytails.

"I'm here to deliver an important package, Mr. Chang. If you could just let me in and sign for it that would be great."

The courier spoke with my partner's voice— the familiar alto, punctuated by the idiosyncratic pronunciations that I found so compelling. I pinched myself, as one does, but this accomplished nothing. One thing was clear to me, though: this person would not set one foot in my apartment.

"I'm sorry, but I'm not gonna let you in. What the hell is going on? Are you Keira?"

Pause.

"It doesn't really matter if I am or not, Mr. Chang. I need to deliver this package— that's my job, and that's what I'm going to do. So if you could please let me in, we can get this over with and you can go back to sleep."

A hot sensation trickled down the back of my head and neck. And something else happened too: I had an erection. I wasn't the least bit aroused, but in this moment I found myself growing inexplicably stiff. Returning my gaze to the peephole, I was unnerved by the courier's unyielding stare; she might have been a statue. I cleared my throat.

"Um, who sent this package?"

"I did."

Right.

"So then, you know what's inside?"

No answer. I felt like I was on a train with no conductor, hurtling deeper and deeper underground and veering off into a hidden tunnel that led to the center of the Earth. Or outer space. Maybe those two things are, in fact, the same. I looked away from the peephole and held my crotch through my white underwear.

"Listen, there's something really strange going on. Are you Keira or not?"

Meanwhile, the person I knew as Keira rolled over noisily in bed and murmured something about red curtains. I looked back toward the bedroom and saw her tossing and turning in the tangle of sheets. The courier spoke up.

"As a matter of record, the girl in your dream never fantasized about you. She gave you her time because she thought you had a good heart. But the truth is, she felt sorry for you, and she was always more interested in your teacher."

I had never mentioned this particular, unrequited episode to anyone. Did this person have access to my dreams? I can't say why I accepted the courier's word, but she was strangely persuasive. Squinting through the peephole, I clutched my swollen erection, which by now had reached feverish proportions. I tried to speak, but all I could manage was a faint hiccuping sound. The courier stepped in obligingly.

"But I'm not here to crush your fantasies, Mr. Chang. You and I know each other too well for such petty squabbles."

We did?

"So... you *are* Keira?"

"Like I said, whether or not I'm really Keira is unimportant. I am and I'm not. You'll have to decide that for yourself."

"Why do you call me 'Mr. Chang'?"

"What else should I call you?"

"Well, you could use my first name, like Keira would."

"I'd rather not."

"Why not?"

Outside, the moon feigned indifference but secretly hung on to every word of our exchange. Even the moths seemed to be listening in.

"Mr. Chang, if you just let me deliver this package you'll find out what you need to know. It's from me— you have to trust me. That is to say, her. However you want to think about it."

"If you know what's inside, why don't you just tell me what it is?"

"Because, Mr. Chang, I don't know what is inside. *She* does. Unless you accept this delivery and open the package yourself, it might get lost. It needs you."

I leaned my forehead against the door, my right palm resting idly next to the peephole.

"So what's it going to be, Mr. Chang? Are you going to let me in? I can't stand out here all night."

All I wanted was to go back to bed— and, with any luck — continue the erotic tragicomedy from which I'd been ejected. But deep down, I knew that the moment had passed; trying to dive back into that world of lost hypotheticals would be like trying to retrieve a spent ripple on a silent lake. Besides, I knew now that my co-star felt nothing for me but a modicum of pity.

"Um, give me a minute."

I stole back to my bedroom, which was still bathed in the half-moon glow. As before, my partner was deafeningly asleep. There was something eery and unnatural about the depth of her slumber, I realized. She wasn't just asleep: she was somewhere else. In one last attempt to wake her, I shook her naked shoulders and murmured hysterically.

"Wake up, Keira, wake up please. There's someone at the door, you've got to help me. Come on, please get up."

But it was no good. Her breathing was noiseless and serene. In a daze, I wandered back to the front door and looked fearfully through the peephole. The courier was still there, grilling me through the tiny glass lens. I withdrew and glared at the peephole from about a foot away, fear and curiosity dancing an aggressive tango in my gut, spilling out into my extremities and setting them a-jitter.

"I'm sorry, I can't let you in. Please just leave and let me go back to bed."

Of course, I wanted to know what was in the package. But if I opened that door, I might be prying open a gateway between truth and delusion— and who knows what might result from the ensuing contradiction. If the world in this apartment and the world on the other side of the peephole represented parallel lines, then my front door was a crossing at infinity; an impossible convergence of the seen and unseen. And the courier was a stray asymptote wandering dangerously close to the axis of my life, which remained stubbornly out of reach but for the proverbial doorway of my apartment. Such doors, I thought, should only be opened in dreams.

A long pause followed, during which I noticed that my erection was practically on the verge of climax despite a conspicuous lack of arousal. I gripped it with a sweaty hand, the tension so acute that I closed my eyes and actually winced in pain. Finally, the courier broke the silence.

"Ok then, Mr. Chang. I can see that you're not going to let me in, and I have other stops to make on my route. I'm disappointed, but I've done my best. I'm going to leave the package right here outside your door, and then I'll be on my way. You can pick it up when I leave or wait until morning, but be careful: the moment passes quickly, and in the morning your doorway may be just a doorway."

I tentatively pressed my left eye to the peephole. The courier was bending down, lowering the package onto my stoop. Then she stood up straight and looked through the glass as before, except now she was empty-handed and clasped her fingers behind her back.

"I'll be going now, Mr. Chang. Have a good night."

I waited for her to leave, but she just stood there. Then she cleared her throat and added:

"Good luck."

Through the peephole, I saw her turn around and descend the short flight of stairs to the street. She walked like a robot, with stiff, standardized steps that carried her into the darkness, tapping echolessly against the pavement. When I could no longer hear her footsteps, I stepped away from the door and leaned my back against it, perspiring. My erection was deflating rapidly, and I realized dully that I was going to have to change my underwear. After I'd caught my breath, I collected myself and unlocked the deadbolt. Then I put my hand on the knob, turned it clockwise, and slowly opened the front door.

To my dismay— or relief, I couldn't tell— the package was there, perched on the top step of my stoop below the door. I picked up the cardboard box with both hands and examined each of its surfaces. There was no writing or markings of any kind. The box was slightly larger than a grapefruit, and it hardly weighed anything. It could have been empty, for all I knew. An empty box, I thought to myself. How moronic that would be.

Stepping back inside my apartment, I shut the door and locked it. Part of me wanted to rip open the package right there, but something told me I needed to wake my partner and tell her everything. Then, we'd inspect this dubious object and make sense of the madness together. When I turned around, however, I noticed something peculiar: my bedroom door was closed. Hadn't I left it open after I tried to wake Keira? Strange. I shuffled up to the door, turned the wobbly knob and pushed it open.

Keira was gone.

Our bedsheets were in their usual state of disarray, fresh drool stains on the pillows under the soft glare of the half-moon. I put the package on the bed and looked around the room, feeling dizzy.

"Hello?"

I called out to her any number of times, but nobody answered. Following the panic playbook, I ran out into the tiny living room and did a sweep of the bathroom and kitchen— but this was, of course, pointless. I went back to my bedroom and sat on the sagging mattress. Instinctively, I reached for the package and held it in my lap. I found myself sitting with my legs crossed, gently cradling the small cardboard box with both hands. Then I turned it over and used my thumbnail to break the duct tape around the seams, severing the adhesive until the top of the box fell open like a wilting flower.

Inside, there was a single piece of paper folded into a square. I took it out, put the empty box aside and unfolded the note. A continuous block of text written in a familiar hand filled exactly one side of the sheet:

I would tell you where I am, but right now, I can't. It's not that I don't want to. I want to tell you, more than anything. But the truth is, I don't know how.

A doorway opened, and I stepped through it— thinking it was only our door. But once I passed through, I found myself in some other place. Everything looks the same, but I don't recognize any of it. I hold your face in my mind, trying to remember. You're having trouble remembering, too. It's like we're only strangers, again.

If you decide to open the door, maybe we'll meet again. But nothing is certain. Even if we do meet, there's no guarantee that we'll be in the right place. In the meantime, I'm supposed to deliver something. I'm scouring the whole city: every street, every mailbox. I may spend the rest of my life trying to find the address. If I'm not careful, this package might become just another piece of dead mail.

It's up to you— the door is there. Miss you. Until next time.

Keira

I put down the letter and looked out the bedroom window, the pale moon floating high above the craggy skyline. In the distance, a gaudy neon panel advertised the Empire Hotel in enormous red letters from the 26th floor. Maybe I should go there, I thought wearily. There was something appealing about the tacky monstrosity that had cropped up in the heart of an otherwise unassuming part of town. I knew I had to leave this apartment, and I didn't know when I'd be back. No destination came to mind, but the Empire Hotel seemed like a good place to start. There was an all-night karaoke bar there, apparently.

My thoughts turned languidly to the dream I'd been having before the courier arrived. But I could no longer picture myself playing the lead role; the girl was still there, but I kept turning into our high school teacher. I closed my eyes, and this sleazy projection became nothing more than a low-budget performance in the theater of my mind.

In the morning, your doorway may be just a doorway.

I folded the letter and put it in my pocket for safekeeping. Then I grabbed my backpack and filled it with some clothes and a few other essentials. I also put on a new pair of underwear. After making a last sweep of my lonely nest, I donned a thin black sweater, old jeans and a pair of battered sneakers. Then I walked to the front door, unlocked the bolt, and opened it slowly. The sun was hours away. I could not know in which realm I now resided, but according to the echoes of a great love and the words of a strange visitor, there was only one way across the chasm. I slipped outside and closed the door. Somewhere, a courier was making the rounds on a transdimensional circuit. I turned the lock and pocketed the key. My first steps through the infinity crossing would be guided by moonlight.

FLESH AND BLOOD

Hair, coiffed. Earrings, matching. Lipstick, vulgar and excessive. Heart, in check. Everything's in order— freshly groomed and ready for delivery. She's Lillie by night, and nobody by day. Cursing the stilettos eating her feet, she steadies her breathing and knocks three times. Tired bedsprings creak to life and precisely six footsteps are heard, each louder than the one before it. The door opens into a sad hotel room. A nondescript male stands at the threshold, stubby black hair and ruffled white dress shirt not quite tucked in. Mid forties.

"Hi, please come in."

Lillie smiles. She goes in for the European one-two kiss, but the man bashfully demurs, lowering his gaze to the floor.

"My name is, uh, it's George."

He closes the door and bows slightly. Then:

"Uh well, actually... it's not," he admits. "I... I guess I don't wanna use my real name. Like, that's what people do right?"

He looks up at her hopefully.

Peering down from her heels, Lillie hides her disgust behind a non-expression. Even without the heels, she's taller than George.

"Nice to meet you, George. My name's Lillie."

She places her handbag next to the lampshade. The deep red curtains are shuttered suggestively.

"So first, payment."

George shuffles over to the desk by the TV and fumbles with his wallet, producing the requisite fee in a crisp stack of bills; withdrawn for this night only. Lillie counts them and stows them in her handbag. Then she assumes her position on the bed and begins to disrobe, peeling off each article of clothing without ceremony. Running a nervous hand through his hairline, George mutters something under his breath. Then he coughs, chokes on himself, and sits down heavily in a chair opposite. He stares at the floor and taps his foot.

"I actually... I was wondering if we could do some role play."

Leaning back on the bed, Lillie eyes him attentively.

"Of course. Whatever you like."

What ghoulish fantasies live inside this terribly ordinary man? Lillie ran through her catalogue of scenes. The humiliated student? The mechanic? Exploited secretary? Kidnapping?

"I'd like you to hire me as your whore."

"Hire you..."

"I want you to... purchase my services for the night. You're my client, and I'm a high class gentlemen for the ladies."

Lillie considers. Recent engagements had included step sister, actual sister, lifeguard, and porcupine. But client? This is a first.

"Just so I understand— you want to be the 'professional' and I'll play the 'customer'? Is that it?"

Fidgeting, George throws a sideways glance at the wall.

"Yes, yes. Uh, yeah that's it. Right. Um."

He fumbles around his pants pockets and pulls out a business card which he holds out to Lillie without looking at her.

```
         GEORGE LI
          ESCORT
       (917) _05 1993
```

The typeface is classy, engraved on expensive card stock that reads money. Svelte, and firm to the touch. Lillie studies the card, and flips it over. On the back, it reads:

WOMEN DESERVE BETTER

Choking back a laugh, she leaves the card on the bedside table and smiles to herself.

"I see, Mr. Li. Well, how should we start?"

"I'm going to get changed, and uh, I actually brought something for you... for you to wear."

George rises abruptly, takes something from the closet and lays it on the bed. It's a long black dress with sleeves, simple yet elegant. It looks old— clean and well-looked after, but definitely used. Someone else's dress.

"After we've both changed, I'll uh, well I'll leave the room and knock on the door. Then you'll let me in and pay me, just like what I did for you, and then... then we'll get started."

"Pay you?"

"Oh, right, of course."

Flustered, George takes his wallet from the desk and fishes out a second wad of bills. The total amount is considerably higher than what George paid *her* for *actual* services rendered. She registers this with an inward snicker and pockets the dummy cash.

"So I'll just give you this when you come in?"

George folds his hands near his crotch.

"Um, actually, why don't you just give it to me at the end?"

You're obviously not in the business, Lillie thinks privately. Every newbie knows that payment is made up front, always.

"Sure, as you like."

"Ok. I'm going to get changed first, uh, in the bathroom. Can you keep your eyes closed until... you know... I've finished and I go into the hallway?"

"As you like."

"Starting now, please."

Lillie closes her eyes while George readies himself. When the room's front door clicks shut, she opens her eyes and picks up the black dress. Following her instructions, she sheds her own uniform and slithers into this curious garment. It fits nicely; an achingly modest piece of attire compared to her usual threads.

"Hello— um, are you ready?"

George's voice is audible from the other side of the door. Lillie adjusts her earrings.

"Yes, I'm all set."

There's the sound of a throat clearing, a recalibration. Then comes three knocks, bold and crisp. For a moment, Lillie is struck with the notion that someone else is knocking.

"Coming."

She walks to the door and opens it. Standing before her is someone who looks just like George— but something is different. This person bows, hands clasped, and fixes her with a refined expression she had not thought possible from this weasel of a man. She's momentarily speechless.

"Good evening, madame. My name is George. I'll be your companion for the night, if what you see is to your liking."

His voice is a full octave lower than the nervous tenor of five minutes ago; this *new* man is, simply, an altogether different person. George's hair is combed stylishly to one side with a discreet, roguish touch, complementing a slim two-piece Armani suit. A silver Rolex completes the effect.

"Oh! Ah, yes, of course— please come in. I'm... I'm Lillie, by the way."

"You look ravishing tonight, Lillie. I hope we'll have a grand time together."

He tops off the compliment with a kiss on the back of Lillie's hand— a light peck, delivered with the easy confidence of a young aristocrat. Bewildered, Lillie has to remind herself that she too is acting— though, admittedly, it would be hard to top this man's performance. She manages a winning smile.

"I'm sure we will. You're... you're more than what I'd hoped for."

"I'm so glad to hear that. Please, relax. Let me take care of you tonight."

He gestures towards the bed and Lillie sits down. George removes his watch, places it noiselessly on the desk, and takes his place next to Lillie.

"So, miss. How may I please you this evening?"

For a moment, Lillie is nonplussed.

"Mmm, well, maybe we could start with a massage..."

The truth is, she *could* use a massage. Consecutive shifts at the Smut-o-Matic XXX night prowl had left her stiff and sore, with no relief other than a troubled sleep. Her tireless hustling provided a means to support herself and her young son, but these days it was becoming harder to define the boundary between her secret career and real life.

"With pleasure, madame. I happen to be a licensed masseur. We can start with the shoulders."

As it turns out, George makes good on his promise: he *is* an expert masseur. Positioning himself behind Lillie (after stripping off his suit jacket, revealing taut muscle contours that had gone previously unnoticed), he places his hands on her shoulder blades and begins a slow rotation with expertly-applied pressure. Lillie's entire body begins to quiver. Wow, I'm in luck, she thinks to herself. Without letting her guard down, she allows herself a tentative moment of repose; her tired back and legs slowly lulled into a state of reassurance they had long ago forgotten.

"So, would you like to tell me about yourself?"

Confessionals are a timeless feature of the terrain, and Lillie happens to be a veteran listener. Most women are, unwillingly. When men probe her for clues about her *other* life, she lies her way through the fantasy with a smile— careful to never reveal a single detail which might collapse the space between her two realities. But suddenly finding herself on the other side— albeit with a strange twist— she feels strangely compelled to spill the beans. She struggles to keep her cover intact.

"Well, you know, I'm... erhm, I'm studying business right now."

This is what she usually told her clients. But it suddenly sounds absurd, a painfully unsuitable narrative. Being a gentleman (or at least pretending to be), George does not challenge her story.

"Mmm, that's very interesting. What sort of business do you plan to go into?"

He may have been bored stiff, but his buttery tone is plenty convincing. Whatever Lillie's imaginary business prospects are, George wants to know about them. Playing coy, Lillie searches for a rejoinder.

"Mmm, the black market."

"Sounds dangerous."

"No more dangerous than your line of work."

"Oh, how's that?"

George cups Lillie's shoulders and gently directs her down onto her stomach. Once she's flat on the bed, he rolls up his sleeves and starts working on her back. He is quite talented— even the deep tissue begins to groan.

"Well, I imagine that you must encounter some nasty clients— maybe even violent ones. Or people who don't want to pay. Not to mention diseases. It's a minefield out there."

"Fair point. And you— you're one of the 'good' customers, I suppose?"

"I like to think so. But are there really any 'good' customers?"

"Do you mean, being civil isn't enough? Paid pleasure is irredeemable?"

"Exactly."

Cracking his knuckles, George puts his hands together and applies pressure to Lillie's lower back, near her ass.

"At a certain point, then, a transaction crosses some invisible boundary and someone becomes a whore. Being someone's whore— it's not about sex, in the end."

He crushes uncooperative muscle tension with ease.

"There's nothing special about selling your body. The world is filled with virgin whores. Whoredom begins with a betrayal of dignity— and anyone who traffics in the indignity of others is, in essence, a complicit john."

George's palms had stealthily maneuvered to Lillie's *gluteus maximus* and now massage them through the strange black dress.

Lillie closes her eyes. Nobody had touched her with such tenderness since before her son's father walked out during the night.

"Are you a john?"

Lillie feels the hands leave her body momentarily to the sound of a belt unbuckling.

"We're all johns, and we're all whores, miss. Life has its way with us and pays us with small pleasures. We in turn have our way with life and pay for it in blood. To cope, as it were."

Very suddenly, Lillie feels the hot, panting sensation of a man's face buried in her crotch from behind. George presses his nose and lips hard and harder into Lillie's erotic nerve center, breathing heavily. Is it play, or is it pleasure? Lillie feels a wetness between her thighs, spreading every second. Does a performance— acted to sheer perfection— cease to be performance altogether?

After a time, however, Lillie discerns a peculiar quality to the wetness. It is, simply, *too* wet. Sensing something amiss, she turns over onto her back and sits up. George is balled up at the edge of the bed, sobbing into the cheaply-laundered sheets. Alarmed, Lillie reaches out to console him— from which George shrinks back like a wounded animal. He stumbles onto the floor, drags himself up onto a chair and stares at Lillie with glazed, dilated eyes. The first man is back— or, seen another way, the second man is gone.

"Why are you wearing my... my mother's dress?"

His mother's dress?

"Easy, darling— you told me to wear this, remember?"

Lillie coos soothingly across the room. But the man is somewhere else.

"I... I failed you, Ma. I'm sorry. Your little boy's been bad. Really bad."

He lunges forward and grabs the hem of the dress, bawling into its black folds from the foot of the bed. Lillie, ever the stoic, beats back the urge to recoil in disgust. Then, George abruptly tears himself away and sets about changing his clothes, frantically gathering up his belongings and shoving them into his pockets. Lillie watches, bemused and vaguely alarmed. George shuffles to the door and grips the handle with an unsteady hand.

"I'm sorry."

And then he's gone, and Lillie is alone. Suddenly, she remembers the prop cash— if she didn't return it, this unhinged character might give her trouble later on. She grabs her purse and opens the door, glancing down the pallid hallway in both directions. But George is nowhere in sight. Strange, she thinks to herself. The elevator is too far: he couldn't have reached it in the time elapsed. She stares, and the empty hotel corridor stays empty.

She returns to the room and lies down on the bed, taking this rare moment of calm. She's still wearing the black dress, which is strangely comforting. Whoever wore this dress was full of love. The last half hour plays and replays on loop, like a screensaver on a computer. Was he even real? She rolls over on her side and gets a half-answer:

GEORGE LI
ESCORT
(917) _05 1993

In his haste to flee the scene, George had forgotten his "business card".

WOMEN DESERVE BETTER

Lillie considers. Then she stands up, turns off the lights and opens the curtains. The moon is visible through a pack of clouds. She takes her phone, exhales, and dials the number on the front of the card. Will it ring?

It does, three times. Someone picks up after the third ring. There's no voice at first— only the sound of shallow breathing. After a moment, Lillie ventures:

"Hello?"

"Hi, Ma."

The familiar, charismatic bass of the other man.

"George? Where did you run off to?"

"I'm sorry, Ma. This was the only way I could reach you."

"It's okay baby. Can Mommy make it up you?"

"Will you do something for me?"

"Anything for you, baby."

"Are you still wearing the dress?"

"Yes."

"I want you to take it off."

Holding her phone against her neck, Lillie peels off the black dress and lays it neatly on the bed.

"It's off now."

"Take a good look at the moon for me."

Lillie walks over to the window. The night sky is overcast, veiling the full moon behind a curtain of clouds.

"There's a cloud around the moon tonight."

"From where I am, I can see the moon perfectly."

"And where is that? Where are you right now?"

"Another time, another place."

In the absence of moonlight, Lillie's naked body glows from within.

"Good bye."

The line goes dead.

For a long time, Lillie simply holds the phone. Then she puts it down, takes a pack of cigarettes from her bag, and smokes. It isn't yet time.

She'll have to go home eventually, back to a wayward son.

But until then, she has other appointments.

CODA

My upstairs neighbor is a famous musician. I have no other neighbors; our building is a crummy duplex from the turn of the century, one apartment per floor. Mine rests at ground level, while she occupies the second floor. A zoning blunder left this building wedged between two commercial towers in the heart of the city: an office complex and a clothing retailer. This rare happenstance leaves us free to raise all hell until the early hours, without fear of noise complaints— provided that both of us are facing oblivion that night. We're nocturnal creatures, so there are no problems between us.

Her name is Beatrice. We don't speak much, but I gather that she moved here after decades of wanderlust— drifting across borders the way an average person crosses a standard intersection. Even now, she insists, there's no telling where she'll be in six months. This transient lifestyle seems befitting of someone much younger than she: I'm twenty-five, and she recently turned seventy. I was born in the city, but I've never considered living anywhere else. While other people chronicle their various exploits in Patagonia, Malta, Vietnam, or wherever, I can't seem to get beyond Newark, New Jersey— where my grandmother lives. I visited Montreal, once, but that was ages ago.

My neighbor cuts a slovenly figure— something pulled from the Gowanus Canal and left on a clothesline, dangling from someone's fire escape. Her hair is violently overgrown, twisted and gnarly grey. Long sleeves hang down over her wrists, keeping her hands out of view when not called upon to perform. Her pants are baggy and frayed at the hems. An acquaintance of mine once mistook her for a homeless person; one of those shriveled old witches stinking up the neighborhood, dragging around a couple of dirty grocery bags. Difficult to imagine her gracing the concert halls of Europe and Asia, to critical acclaim.

She won't tell me where she was born, or where she grew up. Her face bears no clues— only a world-weary frown designed to fend off conversation. It's as if she'd absorbed the faces of everyone she'd encountered in her lifetime of travels, making it impossible to pinpoint her origins. In any case, she prefers to remain stateless. Her accent is similarly indeterminate.

At the moment, my neighbor is not home. She's away on tour— from the steppes of Mongolia to northern Japan, with stops in Hong Kong, Vietnam, Singapore, Mainland China, and Taiwan. She left me her whole itinerary on a piece of paper, slipped through my mail slot in a white envelope. The handwritten schedule— barely legible, the ink smeared in ten places— concludes with the following instructions: *Please feed cat. Plants too. Take out trash as necessary, but not priority. Key inside envelope. — Beatrice.*

The first time she did this, I was shocked. There had been no prior warning, no neighborly relations to speak of. Just a note. That time, she'd flown off to Germany for a weeklong engagement with the Berlin Philharmonic. By the time I found the note, she had already left town— leaving me responsible for the lives of her cat and many houseplants. It made no sense— why would she trust me, a stranger? That first time, I'd considered asking our landlord to advise. But in the end, I thought better of it; the man was an unsavory piece of work from Staten Island whom I'd rather avoid at all costs. So I obliged, grudgingly. The cat didn't die, the plants stayed green. That was the first time I saw her piano.

It's a beautiful piece of craft: a Yamaha grand. The rest of the apartment teeters on the edge of squalor— dusty shelves, piles of envelopes, unwashed dishes. But the piano sits apart from the mess. Its keys, polished to a fault, are nevertheless weathered by the touch of countless études, sonatas, nocturnes, concertos, quintets. The body of the instrument is painted black and elegantly varnished, though a few dents and blemishes in the wood betray an exciting life. I'm not a pianist myself, but imagining the smooth, fading wood under my untrained fingertips excites me, somehow. Every time I find myself in that apartment, fumbling with a bag of cat food, the piano seems to call out to me. Come on, just a simple melody will do, it says. Still, I've resisted the urge to touch her precious instrument— so far.

My neighbor's practice routine is, by some measures, unorthodox. The scales begin at around midnight; up, down, up, down. This goes on for about thirty minutes, a repetitive exercise meant to prime the hands for more substantive material. Then she moves on to complex pieces that far exceed my own musical vocabulary; buoyant, grandiose passages that shake the building to its very foundations. A normal session lasts about four hours— generally topping out at 4 AM. She'll occasionally throw in an extra hour at noon, but no more than that. This arrangement— unthinkable within the shoddy, cramped subdivisions of modern apartment living— suits me just fine. I'm generally in bed by 4:30. Don't ask me why; you'd rather not know.

Don't ask me why; you'd rather not know— this was my neighbor's response to a question I asked her when I first moved in. The question was: how did you get that piano into your apartment? The stairwell is far too narrow, the windows too small for a crane operation. A fairly predictable question— innocuous, breezy smalltalk. But for whatever reason, my neighbor wouldn't tell. Don't ask me why; you'd rather not know. I didn't dwell on her evasion. It made no difference to me one way or another; as far as I knew, she could have had the piano teleported into her apartment, or perhaps they built it from scratch in the living room. None of my business.

She's been gone for over a week now. I'll admit: I miss the sound of that grand piano at 3 AM.

*

I've invited my neighbor over for dinner any number of times. No agenda, no Harold and Maude; just a simple dinner between two people. Whatever her reasons, she declined all of my invitations— all except one.

It was my twenty-fifth birthday, five months ago. I'd slipped a note under her door— she disliked knocking, and loathed the sound of doorbells— informing her of the festivities. In reality, there were to be no festivities; I admitted as much in my invitation. Lacking in both friends and close relatives, I would simply be dining alone in my apartment and would she care to join? I expected the usual deferral, or no answer at all. To my surprise, she showed up just as I was putting on some rice.

At roughly 7 PM, I crossed over from twenty-four to twenty-five years of life behind me. We ate a lavish spread of jasmine rice, chicken thighs with soy sauce, garlic and ginger, and some green beans on the side. We hardly said a word to each other the entire meal. Beatrice sniffed each morsel of food suspiciously, altogether devoid of expression. In the end, though, she cleared her plate like a vulture picking apart a roadside carcass. About thirty minutes had passed before she spoke up.

"How old are you now."

Startled by the sound of her voice, I was momentarily at a loss.

"Oh. I'm twenty-five. Now I am, that is. I wasn't until about an hour ago."

Around Beatrice, everything I said sounded doltish and lame; she seldom spoke, so there was no telling what she actually thought of me. In her presence, words seemed to lose their meaning in mid air. They were carefully formed by a joint effort between larynx, brain, and tongue before sailing across the gulf separating one person from another. But before they could reach their target, some invisible barrier would strip away their dignity, layer by layer, until only the naked sounds remained. Like a faulty space vessel passing through Earth's atmosphere, incinerated beyond recognition by the time it crash-lands in the ocean.

"How old am I."

I couldn't tell if she was asking me to guess, to flatter her, or if she really didn't know how old she was.

"Um, I'm not sure. Sixty-two?"

"Seventy."

"Oh really? My dad's turning seventy this year."

This remark made no impression on her. I excused myself to the kitchen and set the kettle to boil. When I returned, Beatrice had helped herself to more chicken and green beans. She prodded her food with one chopstick, hardly looking at me. Like a child, I thought to myself. Then:

"I am concert pianist. You like piano?"

"Oh, for sure. But me, I never played. I did play clarinet in the school band, though..."

Those words died before they left the runway.

"I taught myself how to play 'Hey Jude'. Did it by ear, actually— I was pretty proud of myself."

Beatrice had speared a piece of chicken with her chopstick and was examining it with some interest. I gulped, and hastened to redirect the conversation.

"— but it's nothing like what you do, obviously. I've read about you online— you're a big deal."

No response.

"These days, I'm more into photography. I love music, though."

Worse still.

"Um, so when's your next concert?"

"Next Saturday. Geffen Hall. Playing with Met. Beethoven fifth concerto," she answered immediately.

"Oh, very nice. Where is that? Is that like Carnegie Hall?"

"Not Carnegie Hall. Not near at all. Lincoln Center. Used to be Avery Fischer Hall, before new endowment."

"Ah."

We ate seconds and thirds. When the water had boiled, I prepared two cups of green tea and set them down on the table, careful not to spill any excess. My neighbor did not react— she didn't even ask what kind of tea it was. Happy birthday, happy birthd—

"Ok, I'm going now. Need to study new piece for concert."

She stood up abruptly and turned away from the table, leaving her tea untouched.

"Oh, alright then. Thanks for stopping by!"

"Mmf."

She shuffled to the door, hunched over. She reminded me of the mole people— the underground vagrants camping out in abandoned subway tunnels. Without a word of thanks or well wishes, she left and returned to her apartment upstairs. I sat back down, drank my tea, and then drank hers.

Later that night, she slipped a note under my door. It was a piece of xerox paper with two words written on it: *Happy Birthday.* I tucked this memento away in a draw, and smiled for the first time in weeks.

*

My photographs are nothing special. I started out as an amateur street photographer, documenting the city's many textures and eccentricities. Berenice Abbot, Henri Cartier-Bresson, Daido Moriyama— all early influences. Gradually,

I began to feel cramped by the burden of legacy— of trails already blazed, worn-out subjects. The city itself was changing too, unhappily. The beautiful decay I had once sought out— from the Bushwick warehouses to the backstreets of Chinatown— was being torn down and paved over by the hour. Five Pointz was long gone, graffiti as an art form hijacked by prime realty. Willets Point would soon go, too. As the city proceeded to demolish what was left of my playground, I turned to faces. People, at least, were not yet made of glass.

That's how I landed in the world of portraiture.

I earn a living taking headshots for the aspiring class: entrepreneurs, fitness gurus, actors, and, sometimes, musicians. I don't pretend to understand their lines of work, but I do have an eye for faces. People trust me to capture their essence— or, if necessary, conceal it and create a false one. Nothing profound about my work, but I get it done.

Robert Mapplethorpe, Khalik Allah, Ren Hang— those are real photographers, taking real portraits. To borrow a phrase from the late Anthony Bourdain: I'm just a standup mercenary.

*

My neighbor is back from her tour. I hear her practicing upstairs— it's 1 AM, and she's working through some incomprehensible modern music. Slamming the keys, seemingly at random, forsaking the easy comforts of melody and pulse. I'm editing a few photographs on my computer, sipping a cup of green tea. The cup is a fine piece of ceramic; grey, smooth, discreet. It was a gift from someone I used to date— before, one day, she stopped answering my messages. An engagement photo showed up online sometime later. Holy matrimony: a still life.

As far as I can tell, my upstairs neighbor never has any visitors. For a world-class musician, her monastic lifestyle strikes me as unusual. Even more unusual than her choice of dwelling; someone of her stature, I presumed, would have no problem renting or even purchasing some glamorous loft in a better building. But she chose to be here. Out there, she's a concertizing pianist of international renown. In this building, she's the cat lady with too many houseplants.

Does my neighbor ever seek out male company? Female company? Something in between, above, behind? Perhaps she is asexual. By choice, or by design? These questions rattle playfully around the perimeters of consciousness far into the night.

I've never been to any of her concerts. Ticket prices are out of reach for the likes of me, and I figure I'm getting a free concert every night. The after hours edition— banging away, chiseling form from pure sound. Someday, I'd like to see my neighbor perform in a proper concert hall. But until then, I'm content to let the music reach me through the floorboards while I kick back with a strong brew and retouch my photographs, waiting for daybreak.

The first signs of dawn are four hours away. I'll be asleep before then.

*

In the morning, there's a note under my door. *Require photography services. Please give quote and leave in mailbox. — Beatrice.*

When I'd mentioned my work over dinner, she'd barely seemed to notice. An offhand remark, innocent and quickly forgotten. And now, months later— a professional inquiry? Just like that, I find myself on the verge of a career breakthrough. A famous pianist wouldn't hurt the portfolio one bit.

That same afternoon, I write a courteous reply and slip it through her mailbox. A long shot, maybe, but not beyond the realm of possibility. A timely response, a slightly inflated fee to give a big league impression— and we could be in business.

A week goes by. No word from my neighbor; her practice sessions continue, more vigorous than ever. She must be busy preparing for that concert at Carnegie Hall— no, she said it was Avery Fischer. Wrong again, goes a weary voice. It's the voice of my twenty-four year old self, recently departed, pushed into retirement by a twenty-fifth year. The future, now the slippery present. It's not Avery Fischer, he says. It's Geffen Hall now, haven't you heard? Right, I sigh. But he's already gone.

I decide to watch a documentary about Ryuichi Sakamoto, the composer. He pays a visit to Fukushima, the site of Japan's most recent nuclear disaster, where he finds a grand piano in the wreckage. He has it rescued and restored, claiming that the trauma of the accident has imbued the instrument with a unique sonority. Recordings are made, and a few excerpts play for the viewer. That's when it hits me: this piano sounds just like the piano upstairs. Vertiginous and haunted, like a stone dropping into a bottomless well. Even the happy-sounding passages are heavy with torment. My neighbor's instrument, I suspect, shares blood ties with Sakamoto's radioactive piano.

One afternoon, I receive a very unpleasant phone call from my landlord. He tells me that beginning next month, a crew will begin "essential renovations" on the building which will, regrettably, obligate him to raise my monthly rent by a "reasonable margin". When he names the figure, I tell him that we appear to have irreconcilable differences on the subject of "reasonable" versus "unreasonable" rent increases. Are these "essential renovations" but a naked ploy to kick me out and lure in some sucker from the suburbs— or the feckless child of a third-world business tycoon? My landlord would hear none of it. We scream at one another, and I hang up.

Another night folds, the mayor loses his re-election bid, and the country lurches toward cultural insolvency. Let them eat each other, I say through gritted teeth.

*

News comes in the form of another note on my doormat, buried under a pile of mail. It says: *Please come for tea. 11 PM OK? — Beatrice.*

Several hours later, I show up at her door, and it swings open. Her apartment is a cave of incoherence— this I already know. She invites me to take a seat at her dining table, cluttered with personal effects. Tubes of chapstick, tiger balm, paper clips, a fly swatter, a stack of CD's. A large sheet of paper dangles over the edge of the table, slightly crumpled; upon closer inspection, the words "honorary doctorate" are visible, inscribed at the top. I marvel at the carelessness of it all.

She gets right to it.

"You take photos."

A question, or merely stating a fact? I nod, and blow across the top of my tea mug.

"Yeah, headshots are my specialty. Portraits, you know."

My neighbor is staring across the table, but not at me. I look down at my mug, and realize with some surprise that the National Rifle Association's logo is printed on both sides, flanked by a patriotic gun display. Hers is the same. I can't help myself:

"So, uh, do you shoot?"

"Shoot?"

"I mean, where'd you get the mug?"

"No, someone gave to me."

I want to ask who, but think better of it. Instead, I get back to the business at hand.

"So you're looking for some new photos then?"

The photograph on her website is at least twenty years old. A stylish black and white job, good lighting. Her appearance has been cleverly retouched, airbrushed beyond recognition. It doesn't look anything like her. A painting would have more faithfully captured the subject.

"Yes."

"Great. So do you need headshots? Or something live?"

"Headshots, fine.

I take a tentative sip of tea. It's bitter as death.

"So you're looking for a new portrait for your website or something?"

"I already have promotional headshot. This is another matter."

I glance over her shoulder at the piano out in the living room. A steady tenant in a crumbling building.

"Sure, that's no problem. But what is this for?"

"Personal business. Confidential. Are you uncomfortable with that."

Her face is utterly devoid of expression.

"Uncomfortable? No, not at all. I take the picture, you keep your secrets. Nobody needs to know. One time, I took photographs for an underground sex dungeon— which will, of course, remain anonymous. Keeping secrets is one of my talents— you might say I'm even better at that than taking pictures. Even if I had secrets to spill, I don't know who I'd tell. Friends are hard to find these days. And don't even get me started on family."

I hadn't meant to say any of those things, but my taciturn neighbor drew it out of me— like a black hole pulling interplanetary detritus into the dark. If she heard me, it doesn't show. Her hair hangs down around her shoulders like rotten seaweed.

"Just one photograph. Maybe more, but probably not. No time, no time."

"Well, just let me know. I'm pretty free this month, so we can set something up quickly if you need it soon. Is the fee okay for you?"

She waves away my question.

"Will contact you soon. I see on your website— good photographer."

I raise my eyebrows.

"Thanks. Sounds great. I do have one question, though."

But before I can ask my neighbor why she has chosen me for this job— when she could, presumably, hire some celebrity photographer like Annie Leibovitz— I stop myself. Call it professionalism, tact, upper middle class discretion; something warns me not to jeopardize this unexpected opportunity. I throw the lever at the very last second and change course.

"Why did you— ahem— where is this piano from? It reminds me of another piano I've heard somewhere. The sound, I mean."

"Piano is ok. Lots of problems."

"Right. But, where'd you get it?"

Silence.

"Sorry, never mind. Just curious. Don't know why I asked."

By now, the tea has cooled. I deplete half the cup, and stare distractedly at the NRA logo.

"So... just let me know when you want me to take the photos."

"Maybe next week. I don't know. I don't have time. So busy. Might cancel. Will let you know."

"Alright, then."

"Okay."

That concludes teatime. I bid her goodnight and head back downstairs to my midtown mansion. When I walk in the door, my neighbor is already practicing. I recognize the piece, but can't name it. A real virtuoso number. Lots of notes, falling into space.

*

A few weeks slip by. Our rendezvous falls by the wayside, and life resumes its uncertain flow. In my spare time, I watch movies that make no sense and try not to read the news. It's becoming harder to distinguish one from the other; fantasy feeding reality feeding fantasy, flushed down a demented spiral of gloom.

I keep working, but my mind is somewhere else. My neighbor, too, seems preoccupied: her practice sessions have gotten longer and more frantic, pushing through sunrise and finally giving out at around 6 AM. She seems to have forgotten about her plans to have the piano photographed. Either that, or she found another photographer.

My dreams are plagued by visions of Fukushima— or what I imagine to be Fukushima. A mental projection of the disaster zone; a drone, swooping down from above, impassively monitoring the devastation. It descends toward the contaminated waters. We see a few broken reactors, overturned chairs, hastily abandoned posts. Some kind of karma, maybe. Then we're taken away from the site, pulled into a glide towards something else. We gain and lose altitude, circling another corner of wasteland. We're peering through the window of some functional building— a school? Then we're inside; down one corridor, through a door blasted open. And there, half submerged in the murky floodwaters, is the piano. We hover before it in wonder. It should be sinking into a radioactive swamp; but instead, the piano is floating. Levitating out of the water, suspended in mid-air. Someone's crying— but that's impossible. There are no people here, not even rescue workers; everyone's been evacuated. Still, there's no mistaking that sound.

At this point, I'm convinced that the Fukushima piano and the piano upstairs must be connected.

*

Another week, and my neighbor is back on the road— the west coast, from L.A. to Vancouver. With some measure of envy, I imagine the roadside motels, old growth forests, Mexican takeout, barreling highways. Though she cares little for any of this. *Chamber music. Mostly Brahms. Back on the 27th,* are her only remarks. Holding fast to our informal arrangement, I meekly assume my cat and houseplant duties.

The first few days are unremarkable: I dump the litter box, change the water and set out fresh plates of raw meat. The houseplants are in bad shape; their leaves, withered and dry. I fill a glass with tap water and do the rounds, hoping for the best. Would my neighbor even notice if all of her plants died? I can't say for sure.

Something happens on the fifth day.

It's past midnight— around the time when my neighbor would normally be practicing her scales. She's not due back for another week and a half. I walk up the flight of stairs and open the door to her apartment, whistling some jingle I heard in an advertisement. It was a commercial for the latest phone— packed full of empty promises and dubious new features.

When I step inside, I feel an unfamiliar presence. An intrusion. Someone— something— is not supposed to be here. A draft blows the doorway open before it slams shut behind me. There's no trace of a break-in, no signs of forced entry. Everything is as it should be: piled high, strewn across dusty surfaces.

And then I see it.

She's curled up on the rug. I recoil at the sight of her, knocking over a pile of old vinyl LP's with my elbow and sending them crashing onto the floor.

"Oh, fuck."

I raise both hands in the air and back away, slowly. The woman rolls over, opens her eyes, and stares right at me.

She's a complete mess. Her outfit— a trailing black dress— is torn to pieces and smeared with mud. Long, black hair tangled from follicle to split end upon split end trails down to her shoulders, splaying across the carpet. Bare feet.

Her whole body is drenched, soaked through with dirty water. She must be around my age— mid twenties.

A few scenarios cross my mind, each more absurd than the last. A bum from the street, camping out for the night? An unhurried burglar, taking advantage of the empty digs? Or, just maybe— a houseguest, not only welcome but actually invited by the witchy old pianist herself? Option three looms with troubling plausibility.

Bits of dust and oily residue cling to the tattered fabric of her dress. I know I need to say something, but my brain is offline.

"Hey."

She says something in a foreign language.

"Who are you? What the hell are you doing here?"

I reach instinctively for my phone, tucked in my right hand pocket. My neighbor doesn't have a cellphone, so calling her is impossible. My landlord might know what's going on, but I have no desire to speak to him. 9-1-1 is only a dial tone away. But my grasp of the situation is too vague; bringing in the cops could turn out to be a disastrous miscalculation. What I need is an impartial, aerial view of the multiple curiosities unfolding before me— something to better inform the decisions being weighed, the simulations running through my mind. As things stand, it's simply too soon to know.

Before I can investigate further, my phone buzzes in my pocket. Startled, I answer after one ring.

"Hello?"

"... Hello. This is an automated message. Are you planning to vote in the upcoming federal election? Are you satisfied with the current administration? We value your opinion. Please spare a minute of your time for these important—"

I hang up in disgust, no closer to any kind of decision. The woman looks around, confused. Time is running out. I back out of the apartment and close the door on this dismal turn of events without a backward glance.

Something is happening up there.

I'm down the stairs and halfway to the end of the block. I'd barely reached the McDonald's on the corner before another realization hits me:

The piano had disappeared.

*

Are you satisfied with the current administration?
We value your opinion.
Please spare a minute of your time for...

*

My neighbor's piano was missing, a strange woman on the carpet where the instrument should have been.

There's a connection between the piano and the unknown woman. But she couldn't have stolen the piano. A piano heist is a sophisticated operation; even the best laid plans are prone to failure, vulnerable to any number of unpredictables. No way some ordinary crooks could pull this one off— not even with a team of Dwayne Johnsons. The staircase corridor is not nearly wide enough for the body of the piano, and forget about the windows. They'd have to shear a hole in the roof and remove the instrument with a crane; by the time they cut through, the cops would already be storming the place. I shake my head.

It's one hour later. I'm pacing around my apartment, trying to pull it together. Eventually, I take out my phone and compose a message to my neighbor. By now, she must be playing to a sold-out audience in San Francisco. She rarely responds to emails, but I have no other way to reach her.

```
Dear Beatrice,

I hope your tour is going well. Sorry to bother
you, but if you have a free moment please call me
— it's important, it's about your apartment.

Thank you,

X

P.S. Your plants are looking good. The cat is
eating well, too— looks like he's fattening up
for the winter. No problems there.
```

I send it off and anxiously go to my kitchen for a snack. All I have are frozen bagels, and some old hummus. I throw a bagel in the oven and lay the tub of hummus on my countertop. Then I have a glass of water from the tap.

I'm in serious trouble. Even if the piano's disappearance is not, strictly speaking, my fault— my neighbor would never forgive me for this kind of gross negligence. Whatever tenuous rapport exists between us would end after this, frayed beyond repair. I imagine a future full of rage, threats and litigation.

The piano had vanished on my watch. A hard fact— neither fair nor adjustable. And now, there's a woman squatting in the apartment. Add to this fiasco my recurring dreams about the Fukushima nuclear meltdown, and we've got a Class 1 catastrophe on our hands.

Had I forgotten to lock the door after my last visit? Impossible. The door locks by itself, from the inside. My neighbor forbade me from opening the windows *(Broken. Don't use)* so nobody could have entered that way. One mystery follows another, pulling a hapless private eye into the mounting absurdities.

*

It comes to me some time later, while I'm folding socks and stuffing them into my drawer.

Someone whispers in my ear:

She *is* the piano.

*

The woman is still there, staring straight ahead. I close the door behind me and walk tentatively towards her corner of the room. As I get closer, the smell of sulphur catches in my nose and throat. For a moment, I'm standing on a jetty by the bay— Dead Horse Bay? Ocean rot, and miscellaneous decay. Then I remember where I really am and snap to attention. It's time to toughen up and get some answers.

"Hello?"

I stoop down, keeping my distance. The woman does not react, at first. A few tense moments pass in silence. I'm sweating.

When the woman turns over and looks directly at me, I freeze. Then, she says:

Fukushima.

Scraps, severed threads fall around her shoulders and then the carpet. Some metaphysical joker is having a field day. Who's pulling the strings here?

"What's in Fukushima?"

We look into each other's eyes, trying to understand.

I take my phone from my pocket. Due to a hardware malfunction, it goes straight to camera. The lens points lazily at the woman's bare feet, swaying in time with my shaking fingers.

She's no longer looking at me. Her eyes are drawn to the screen on my phone, and she inches forward to get a closer look. I shrink back apprehensively. She comes right up in front of me, and, very slowly, reaches out with a steady hand. I feel powerless to react; in a moment, she's taken my phone from me and is pointing it around the room. She appears unfamiliar with the technology, but wields it with confidence— like a scientist taking esoteric measurements, or examining a rare artifact. I'm sitting on the floor, legs crossed, doing my best impression of a fire hydrant.

Now she's pointing the phone right at me, holding it at arm's length. I can't see her face, but she can surely see mine.

An incoming call breaks the moment, and the woman drops my phone in surprise. It lands on the carpet by her knees. I swoop forward to pick it up, and my hand brushes hers. It's cold and brittle, grains of sand clinging to the hard skin. When I look up, the room wavers. Our faces are too close now. She smells of brine and mildew.

*

The night muddles through, full of dithering and lust.

"Are you the piano?"

She reclines on the carpet, fulfilling an agenda unknowable to me or anyone else.

*

Some time ago, I'd decided to canvass my neighbor's apartment— looking for clues, trying to understand who this person was, where she was headed. Her home, I discovered, is a chaotic, troubled place. Messy bookshelves were found to contain war volumes, psychology textbooks and photography compendiums with titles like "The Vivisected Mind" and "Famine: 1000 Days and Nights". The postcards and letters stuck to her refrigerator chronicled the many unrequited loves sent her way across oceans and the Trans-Siberian railway.

Dearest Beatrice,

I'm writing this on the longest of nights. Tangiers is terribly lonely, and I find myself thinking of our times together. You were a pure delight on stage; compared with you, Martha Argerich is a total bore. Even Glenn Gould has something to answer for, as long as you're around. I only wish we could have had more time to ourselves: you have so many stories, and I want to hear every single one of them. Seems I'll have to wait for your return to London, or perhaps I should make an impromptu visit to New York. I heard it's terribly cold over there. Stay warm, sending love from these exotic shores. Until next time, then. —

Charles

Beatrice,

Greetings from Hong Kong, the city of neon. I'm here on business— no, who am I kidding, it's a vacation. I thought of you, our night spent here together, and how I wish I could relive it over and over. From the first moment I saw you perform, I knew I had to meet you. I remember it well: it was an all-Chopin concert at the Lee Theatre, no intermission. You were just passing through, as was I. We had a few drinks, and then you went home. I begged you for your address so that I could write you, and to my relief you agreed. So, here I am. I apologize for being so clumsy with my words... I was never so eloquent. Hoping this reaches you. Warm regards, Stanley

Béatrice, je compte les jours depuis notre dernière rencontre... deux mois déjà !

Aujourd'hui je me baladais dans le 14ème et mes pas m'ont guidés, un peu par hasard, devant le café Intermède. Ton image s'est tout de suite imposée à moi. Des détails de notre rencontre me sont revenus en mémoire... Tes mains si fines et élégantes, autour de cette tasse de café noir. Sans lait ni sucre.
Vivre la vie que je mène, celle d'une femme qui ne désire que d'autres femmes, n'est pas toujours facile. Mais je ne t'apprends rien, je crois. C'est vrai qu'il y a déjà quelques personnes dans ma vie en ce moment. Ce sont de belles distractions mais je ne parviens pas à t'oublier, Béa. Tu me plais. Non pas seulement comme musicienne mais aussi, et surtout, en tant que femme. Penses-tu que l'on pourra se revoir bientôt ?

Je t'embrasse,
Ondine

A tour of the kitchen proved bewildering: it was full of cooking appliances, but conspicuously lacking in comestibles. My neighbor, by her own account, prefers takeout. The pantry was packed full of Ichiban instant noodles, stacked up to the ceiling. Above the stove, her liquor cabinet boasted an impressive collection of hard spirits; European and Japanese imports, mostly, fronted by a large bottle of absinthe. It was three-quarters empty that time, as were the rest. Fuel for the long road, I suppose.

The apartment was full of plants. Every shelf, windowsill and table played host to a variety of flowers, bonsai and humble cacti— half of them dead, the other half on the outs. I did my best to revive the dead ones, dousing them with water and clicking my tongue in sympathy. Helpless victims of a life lived in caprice.

In the bathroom, I found a tiny weed growing out from the crack between tiles. Hardy and brash, it seemed determined to persist in the face of overwhelming odds. This was no ordinary patch of mold or urban dandelion; the stem was thick, with bottomless roots holding on for the long haul. Incredibly, it's still there today— I've taken to watering it like all the other plants. It never seems to grow any bigger, though.

*

I'm dreaming now. The scene is dark, heavy with tragedy. It is not my tragedy, and yet I feel somehow accountable. A grand piano is floating— just floating— in a classroom destroyed by the flood. My own position is undefined; all I have is the vision before me, observed from a disembodied pair of eyes.

Someone is swimming toward the piano from across the room. A rescue worker? A student left behind in the ruins?

It's my upstairs neighbor.

I try to yell, but no sound comes and she keeps swimming. When she reaches the piano, it is no longer a piano: the young woman on the carpet has taken its place. My neighbor takes the young woman on her back, like a lifeguard, limp arms wrapping loosely around the older woman's neck. She begins to swim away— laboriously, now — single-mindedly heading for the doorway. I try shouting again; my neighbor takes no notice.

And then, she's drowning.

The girl has vanished, and my upstairs neighbor is being crushed by the full weight of the grand piano. It's pushing her down into the condemned waters, no longer floating. The old woman makes no move to escape: despite everything, she's still trying to save the sinking piano. She's fully submerged now, pushing and grasping in vain at its slippery body. Her hands strike the keys, producing a limp cacophony of sound. The tip of the piano sticks above the dirty water like an iceberg.

She's not going to make it, I realize. Water levels are rising, bits of dirt and plastic bobbing across the agitated surface shimmering with toxic runoff. I want to dive in and pull her out, but I have no body here: the scene is filtered through pure (un)consciousness, placidly observing from the sidelines. I know it's a dream, but it is no less real. My neighbor is still clawing at the keys, but it is no longer random: a melody reaches me from below the waves. It is a melody composed of unrealized emotions, nostalgia from somebody's future. The flood has almost reached the ceiling; I have nowhere to go. I'm underwater now, and I see my neighbor— her long hair suspended in motion, hunched body pinned to the floor, hacking at the keys and expelling bubbles with every breath, mere seconds from death. She turns, we see each other for an instant. Then the lid of the piano slams shut, and the room goes dark.

*

When I wake up, I'm drenched through. My clothes reek, particulate matter scratches my eyes from under their lids. Everything hurts, and I'm coughing into a damp carpet.

"Hello."

I roll over.

"Got back one hour ago. Bad traffic."

She doesn't seem the slightest bit surprised to see me. Satisfied that I'm not dead, my neighbor shuffles around the apartment and drags a chair into the kitchen for no apparent reason. The back of my hand knocks against a hard, smooth surface.

I sit up with some difficulty, making sure not to bang my head on the underside of the piano. Then I stand, slightly dizzy, inspecting the rematerialized— and apparently undamaged—instrument. Not a trace of water or scuffing. The young woman is nowhere to be seen.

My neighbor is pouring herself a drink. I join her in the kitchen and stand beside the pantry. She offers me a glass of something hard, and I accept. It's bitter, aged for a thousand years.

"Someone gave to me, many years ago."

I nod, listlessly. Was it Stanley, or Charles? Ondine?

"What day is it today?"

"Thursday. 27th."

I close my eyes. I was out for three days? Impossible.

"The 27th? No way."

I take my phone from my pocket, but it appears to be dead. Water drips from the power socket onto the kitchen floor. Where was I just now?

We drink in silence. The sound of a crane pulverizing another city block sends a tremor through the room. My neighbor's face is lost in a tangle of hair, her eyes hidden behind a thick pair of glasses. She looks like a goldfish.

When we've finished our liquor, she abruptly leaves the kitchen and scurries over to the piano. Her long sleeves brush the keys as she sits down and launches, without ceremony, into her practice routine. It's a miracle that her fingers don't snag on the loose fabric hanging about her wrists; unbothered, she runs her scales at breakneck velocity, then does them again at half the speed. I place my empty glass in the sink and slowly creep out into the living room, taking one last look at the piano before I open the door to leave.

"Thanks for the drink."

She doesn't respond— she's completely forgotten that I'm even here. I unlock the deadbolt, pull open the door, and slip out onto the stairs. The scales have resumed their virtuoso brilliance, zipping up and down the piano keys the way a convertible traverses a familiar highway. I return to my apartment, strip off my wet clothes, and take a long shower. Something is happening, something beyond me and my simple life. Soapy runoff trickles down my back, my legs and swirls into the drain. Upstairs, the scales run up and down, audible through the sound of water.

*

The next few months pass uneventfully. A few gigs trickle in, none of them very interesting. Autumn gives way to winter, the dead leaves frozen in place and buried under a thin layer of frost. My neighbor keeps practicing, but doesn't get in touch. Our photoshoot has been put on indefinite hold.

To fill the space between jobs, I try meeting people. Some encounters are passionate enough, but without depth. Following the old cliché, I fall into a brief and tempestuous affair with one of my clients— a dancer at the Alvin Ailey School named Soren. Our first night together, she tells me that she has a boyfriend overseas.

"Oh. And we are— is this— okay?"

"Not really, no. I guess I'll have to tell him."

"That's one way of looking at it."

We keep on seeing each other, sending off a flirtatious message when the mood strikes. One snowy evening in February, we're lying in bed, her fingers tapping my chest to some beat that only she can hear. My neighbor is practicing her scales upstairs.

"Does she always practice so late?"

"Yep. Not before 11, usually. And never before 10."

"Does it bother you?"

"Nah, it's fine. Actually, I really like hearing her play— it's comforting, like having a guardian angel upstairs. As long as she plays the piano, it keeps the bad energies away."

"She's a pretty big deal, you know. I read about her after the first time I came over."

"Yeah, she's famous. What you didn't read, though, is that she used to live in a brothel when she was living in Germany, back when she was young."

"What? You mean she was a—"

"No, she wasn't one of the girls. She just needed a place where she could practice her piano— she'd had lots of problems with neighbors and landlords. She'd just gotten kicked out of her apartment, and one of her friends happened to be a part-time prostitute. So I guess she connected the dots, and just moved in. Nobody gave her any trouble."

"That's craaaaaazy. It didn't bother her?"

"She said she loved it. Well, what she said was—"

I imitate my neighbor's deadpan grumble:

"Good apartment. Could play piano all night. No problems."

Soren laughs.

"I wonder if I have that much dedication. To dancing, I mean."

"You're at a top dance school."

"That's not what I mean. I know I'm good— but what does dancing really mean to me? Can I live without it? Should I be able to live without it? What's even the right answer to that?"

"So you're wondering, would you have been able to live in a brothel for the sake of dancing?"

"Exactly. And I'm not sure if I would. So what does that make me?"

"It makes you a reasonable human being."

"I can't help but feel like being reasonable is a kind of mediocrity."

I'm at a loss for words, and we let our thoughts slide. Eventually, she says:

"I'm going out of town for a few weeks."

"Really? What for?"

"I need a vacation."

"That sounds like a good idea."

I let out a long sigh.

"Huh. Well, I'll miss you."

She makes no reply, but traces a line across my stomach with the tip of her finger. Her arm is pure sinew, sculpted to perfection by years of dancing. Out of nowhere, she says:

"You know, nobody wants to see a woman with real muscle."

I bury my nose in her dark brown hair.

"What do you mean?"

"Even in movies like Wonder Woman, they had to pick someone who looks like a Victoria's Secret model. If they cast a real athlete— someone ripped, like Serena Williams, the tennis player— nobody would watch it. It sucks, but it's true."

"Unfortunately, I think you're right. People aren't there yet."

"Will they ever be?"

"I try to stay optimistic."

"Would you see a movie like that?"

I gently squeeze her shoulder. Hard as kevlar, limber as the branch of a willow in springtime.

"Of course. I mean, if the story was good."

She's silent for a time. Then:

"Will you come with me?"

"Come with you where?"

"To Japan."

"What?"

"My boyfriend is there. That's where I'm going."

"Your boyfriend?"

Being reasonable is a kind of mediocrity.

"So you guys are still together, then."

"Well... sort of. We're keeping things open."

"The motto of our generation."

"What is?"

"'Keeping things open.' We were told we could be rock stars in kindergarten, so we're 'keeping things open' just in case we hit it big one day."

"Uh, okay..."

She pinches the flesh between my thumb and forefinger. I run the back of my other hand over the tiny wisps of hair on her arm.

"So anyway, this 'vacation'..."

"Yes?"

"Why should I come with you?"

"I don't want to be alone."

"You won't be alone. Not for long, anyway— I'm sure your boyfriend will be happy to see you."

Upstairs, my neighbor is bulldozing through an acrobatic piano passage. She's played this one a million times.

"Oh come on. Don't you need a vacation too?"

"Hm. In a way, I'm always on vacation. So I don't know..."

"When was the last time you left the city?"

"Let's just say it's been a while."

"So why not come with me? It might inspire your photography. And anyway, it's so cold and shitty here right now. How can you stand it?"

"I don't know. Which part of the country are you headed for? Tokyo?"

"No, not Tokyo. My boyfriend lives in Fukushima."

The windows rattle faintly, rent by a frozen gust of wind. I take a deep breath.

"Okay, I'll come."

"Really? I was sure you'd say no."

"I was going to, but circumstances have changed."

"'Circumstances have changed?' And what would those circumstances be, exactly?"

I kiss her, and we pass feverishly through the crucible of desire. There's no telling where this fatal attraction is taking us; we give ourselves in full, careful not to question or smother it. This might not be love, but for now, it's close enough.

*

Two weeks later, I've packed a small suitcase with clothes and toiletries. I've never been to Japan before, and know almost nothing about the place. All I've got are watered-down impressions from movies and restaurants, and a few dubious testimonials from friends. Before I leave, I slip a note under my neighbor's door informing her of my departure.

Hi Beatrice. I'll be away for a few weeks, just so you know. I guess you can call it a vacation— though I'm not sure what it is, to tell you the truth. Everything is so muddled, I just need to get out of here and clear my head. Anyway, sorry for ranting— will let you know when I return. Hope you're doing well, and maybe we can have tea when I get back... Cheers — X

My doorbell rings, and I head downstairs where the dancer is waiting for me.

"Ready?"

I nod. We head for the subway, transfer to the A train, and ride it all the way to the airport. Security is congested and slow, but there's no trouble. I check my suitcase and we wander through the food court, marveling at all the trendy new kiosks. Poké with tataki. Spicy Xi'an noodles. Pizza à la margarita. The ghosts of frozen hot dogs and canned soup fade into history, no match for this millennium. We share a pizza and browse the airport bookstore. I read a few pages of Malcolm Gladwell before replacing the book on the shelf without buying it. The cashier gives me a dirty look, and I shrug helplessly.

A few hours later, we're on the plane. Soren reads a paperback while I scroll through the in-flight cinema. Mind-numbing action flicks and cheap comedies abound, but there's a documentary channel too. To my surprise, the film about Ryuichi Sakamoto sits at the top of the list.

I decide to watch it again. When the drowned piano appears, I feel short of breath; I grip my armrest until my fingers hurt, a cold sweat breaking out on my chest and forehead. The peeling body of the instrument parades before me on the small, outdated screen, wretched and seductive. I take a closer look: it's a Yamaha grand. My neighbor's piano is a Yamaha. Could it be? I rewind and play the sequence again. A flight attendant offers me a choice of beverage, and a plastic cup appears on my tray table. I absently sip its contents. Orange juice? Minute Maid. Or is it Minute Made?

Intermittent time checks at 11 PM, 1:32 AM, then 3:05 AM. With the windows shut, these numbers lose their meaning— unmoored from the natural cycle of sleep and wakefulness as we cross many time zones. Soren is out cold; her book, wide open, lying face down on her lap. I try to sleep, but a growing trepidation keeps me awake. What the hell am I doing, I wonder, squirming fitfully in my seat. Hours blur together, blank units without value.

Complementary breakfast rouses me from a troubled half-sleep. It's a stale bread bun with butter and jam, and instant coffee. Soren is already awake and alert, drinking hot coffee while she finishes her book.

"What time is it?"

"Mm. Does it matter?"

"Late, then."

"Early. Doesn't feel like it, though."

"Blgghb."

We begin our descent minutes later. My ears pop, the plane shudders, and we've landed. We enter the terminal, pass through customs and retrieve our luggage. Well dressed locals and shabby tourists mingle in the waiting areas, children diverting themselves on their electronic tablets. I find a food vendor and buy something called a yakisoba dog— a bread bun stuffed with greasy noodles and bright pink ginger shreds. It's surprisingly delicious, but I feel drowsy and unwell: I take three bites and give the rest to Soren.

Our plan is simple. We're spending the night in Tokyo, then taking the train to Fukushima tomorrow morning. She'll join her boyfriend, and I'll go off on my own. When things wrap up, we'll rendezvous back in Tokyo and spend a few days there before flying home together. After that, who knows.

The Narita express train shuttles us from the airport to central Tokyo in just under thirty minutes. Unlike the sputtering, rundown network of subways and buses back home, everything seems to work here. Comic book colors pop out from every sign and billboard, overwhelming the senses with bold proclamations and flashing lights. The tunnels are a sea of black hair, like mine, a conduit for the orderly throngs of office workers. We pack into a crowded train on the circular Yamanote Line, transfer once and ride a commuter line to the comparatively quiet neighborhood of Koenji. An hour later, we leave the subway and a narrow side street leads us to our accommodations— a studio apartment rented out to visitors by some shrewd property owner. We throw down our bags, take a shower, and collapse on the futon in the middle of the room. After our nap, we turn on the electric kettle and boil some water. A selection of tea packets has been conscientiously left out for us on the tiny countertop: green tea, black tea, and what appears to be burdock tea. We opt for green tea, and try to blast our brains awake with multiple infusions. Soren maps out a possible itinerary while we sip our drinks, rattling off names of landmarks that sound exciting but draw little reaction from me. I'm too tired to party.

In the end, we don't make it to the delirious heart of Tokyo. Shinjuku, Shibuya, Roppongi; all that will have to wait. For now, we settle for the classy bohemians in our own neighborhood; the area is alive with record stores and tiny bars, their frontage stylishly painted over with colorful graffiti. I take some photographs of our little village, and a few shots of Soren. Then we stop in a coffeeshop for lunch. An effusive barista serves us black tea with lemon, and Soren orders a donut. This might be the best donut I've ever had, she declares, not offering me a bite. Country music plays softly around us— a gravelly voice, rusty guitar. But then I realize that the words are sung in Japanese; all is not what it seems. The afternoon passes languidly, and I'm very far from home.

*

The next morning, we rise early and vacate the apartment. A long subway ride takes us to an interchange where we board a bullet train bound for Fukushima. We find two seats on the right and sit back, calmly accelerating, frantic glimmers of Tokyo crossing and vanishing from our line of sight beyond the large compartment windows. The skyline gradually thins out, opening onto a well-groomed countryside.

"Will you be okay? Once we get there."

I nod.

"Yeah, I'll be fine. I'll just walk around, take some photos... I'm used to being alone."

A station announcement plays over the loudspeakers, followed by a jingle.

"So what is your boyfriend doing in Fukushima anyway? It's kind of a small town, right?"

"Oh, well he grew up in Japan until he was twelve— he has family here. His dad is American, but his mom is Japanese. So he moved back about a year ago."

"Mhm. It seems very nice here. In Japan, I mean. Even after being here for only a day, I think everything back home seems totally broken and antiquated."

She sighs.

"I know what you mean. This is such a dreamy place."

Someone across the aisle is eating a lunch box full of noodles, slurping them down as if it were a competitive sport.

"You don't have to stay in Fukushima, you know. It's my business to take care of. You should feel free to go see other parts of Japan in the meantime, and we can just meet back in Tokyo after."

"True enough. But I have my own business to attend to in Fukushima, actually."

"Really? You never told me that."

"It's a long story."

"Do you know someone in Fukushima?"

"Yes. Well, no— not exactly. It's hard to explain."

"What. Is some girl there?"

She laughs, and my thoughts gurgle indistinctly. I shake my head and say no more about it. What would my upstairs neighbor think? I picture her at the keys, hammering away at some substantial piece of music beyond my grasp, grumbling in a low voice.

Thanks to our train's superior speed, we cover staggering distances in no time at all. We pull into Fukushima around lunchtime, perfectly on schedule. As the train slows, I grab my suitcase from the overhead compartment and Soren pinches my arm.

"We should get off separately, I think. He might be waiting for me."

"Got it."

"I'll go first."

She smiles, and then she's gone. I follow at a discreet distance, stepping onto the platform and casting around for the exit. I expect to see Soren from the corner of my eye, embracing a strange man. But no such scene appears. In fact, I don't see her on the platform— she must have already gone down the stairs a few feet away. I adjust the straps on my backpack and walk towards the exit as the train doors close. Not long now, I mutter under my breath.

*

Fukushima is an unassuming town. Though life has mostly resumed its ordinary flow since the 2011 nuclear meltdown, memories and radiation still loom large. Wreckage sites remain off-limits, isolated from the inhabited zones supposedly fit for human dwellings. I stop in a 7-Eleven for an egg salad sandwich before taking a cab to my hostel— a seaside boarding house. When I arrive, I leave my suitcase behind the reception counter and pay for the room. Then I head outside and pick a street, more or less at random, before setting off on foot. I'm in no hurry. A few locals pass me on their bikes; I can smell the ocean from here. There's a dusty karaoke joint named "Cherry Bar" just down the road. It's closed at the moment; maybe it'll open for happy hour. Painted entirely in pink, an unlit neon sign spells out C—H—E—R—R—Y   B—A—R in vertical letters. I take out my camera and snap a photograph. A seagull lands on the sign and squawks before flying off again.

I find a spot by the waves and sit down. The truth is, I've never been this far from the City before. Everything I know about the world outside is secondhand, learned vicariously through snapshots of other people's lives. How much of my own experience is truly authentic? Nobody can say. If you live in a dream, is it true by definition? Is wakefulness a kind of exile from dreams— and therefore, a smug denial of truth? I feel my thoughts drifting, pulled out into hazy waters like strands of kelp in the tide.

No news from Soren. That's to be expected— but the pangs of absence hurt nonetheless. I wonder what she's up to.

Afternoon gives way to early evening, cast in a golden hue by the setting sun. I find a local izakaya and take a seat at the counter, alone. There's a menu on the wall, which of course I cannot read. I pull up an internet translator on my phone and type in "noodles". When the chef turns to me, I flip my phone around and show him the screen. He nods briskly, then retreats to the kitchen behind a pair of soft curtains. Minutes later, a bowl of noodles appears, topped with seaweed and a bundle of deep fried vegetables.

I put my hands together— as if in prayer, as I had seen others do— and mutter a sheepish *arigato gozaimasu*, hoping no one can hear me. It's humble food, but it's the best dinner I've ever had. The best donut? The best dinner? What is this place?

By the time I leave the restaurant, dusk is settling in. I walk back to my hostel, retrieve my belongings from behind the desk and head straight to my room. It's small, but inviting. There's a simple bed by the window; I flop down and just lie there for a while. Then I take out my phone, connect to the internet and check my emails. Nothing important; a fundraiser for my high school alumnae association, a promotional discount from booking.com, a notice of renewal for an online cinema subscription. I do the rounds, then turn my attention to the matter at hand.

But, it turns out, there isn't much information about the Fukushima piano to be found. Despite hours of sleuthing, nothing much turns up; a few reviews about the documentary, critical appraisals of Sakamoto's music, various articles about the 2011 disaster— but nothing concerning the piano's current whereabouts, or the exact location of its rescue. Of course, Sakamoto himself must know— but someone like me can't just call him up.

I decide to write to him. Bleary with jet lag, I pull up his website and hastily draft an email to his agent:

```
Dear Mr. Sakamoto,

   I'm a young photographer doing a series on
pianos.  I  recently  watched  your  documentary,
"Coda"— and while I was not too familiar with
your  music  before  now,  your  work  with  the
"drowned" piano from Fukushima deeply moved me.
```

```
I would like to include that particular piano
in my photography series. I was wondering if you
knew where the instrument currently resides— what
is its status? Furthermore, would it be possible
to visit the site (in Fukushima) where you
originally found it? This is all very important
for my work.
    Thank you very much for your time— I would be
extremely grateful if you could help me with this
project.
    Best regards,

    X
```

I send it off without further revision, too tired to proofread. My chances of receiving a response are about as likely as my surviving a nuclear explosion; in any case, I should have done this weeks ago. Overcome with a sudden fatigue, I throw my phone on the mattress and turn over. Sleep comes for me, and I gratefully relent.

*

It's dark when I wake up. I check the time: just after 9 PM. My head feels heavy, and I need something to drink. There are two bottles of water on the desk across from the bed; I take one and drain it in a single gulp. Then I splash some cold water on my face from the sink. There's someone in the bathroom mirror who looks just like me, but I'm not convinced that it's my reflection. A good imitation, I say out loud.

The streets are quiet and calm. I walk in no particular direction, enjoying the sensation of being deliberately aimless. A narrow road, flanked by family homes; the scene isn't exactly riveting, but I find a glorious sense of peace here. Each tiny driveway contains a car— all in glimmering, pristine condition. They look fresh off the conveyor belt from the Mitsubishi factory; their sheen is, if anything, artificially perfect. I see one man kneeling by the tires of his silver Honda, scrubbing the hubcaps with a toothbrush. On the balcony of a neighboring house, someone is taking down the laundry hung out to dry, unclipping the extra large clothespins holding it all in place. I pass a vending machine, thoughtfully placed on a nondescript corner, its intriguing selection of canned coffees and sodas glowing white behind the plastic window display.

I wander around without conviction for a time, taking the occasional photograph but nothing serious. Eventually, I find myself back on the main road— I've done a full circle. A few pedestrians pass me on the sidewalk, including one blond tourist with a fancy camera around his neck. He catches my eye, but I keep walking. The moon, cut in half, floats high above the sea.

At the end of the thoroughfare, I see the Cherry Bar. It appears to be open; the neon sign has been lit, enticing customers off the street with its bright pink lettering. Curious, I head straight for it. A panel below the sign promises drinks, food, and karaoke. The logo— a cherry— seals the deal for me. I stow my camera, open the door, and step inside.

*

The night is in full swing. Elderly customers pack the bar, sipping their drinks and chatting in subdued voices. Occidental memorabilia lines the walls— Campbell's Soup via Andy Warhol, Brigitte Bardot, John Coltrane, the

Brooklyn Bridge. Someone's singing karaoke in the back, an old man alone on a small stage. There's an upright piano off to the side, but nobody's using it.

I take a seat at the counter and order some sake. It arrives promptly, and I raise my glass to nobody in particular. Then I think again, and decide to toast my upstairs neighbor. It takes me a moment to find the words — some phrase celebrating the artist and her years of drifting. To strange lives lived, and a handful of mysteries, I think to myself, taking an enthusiastic swig of sake. As the alcohol seeps into my bloodstream, life's rough edges begin to blur. Some kind of clarity emerges from the narcotic fog — the sort of insight best handled by a pleasantly warped mind. Those afflicted with wanderlust must feel at home only when they're furthest from it. A transient existence is a series of erotic encounters; the place is the affair, loved truly but without sacrifice. For a rootless pianist on the run... where will she go next? This sake is incredible.

The old man finishes his karaoke number, to a round of applause. He bows, and carefully places the microphone back on its stand. Then he rejoins a friend sitting at a table by the stage; they drink ("kanpai!"), laugh, and drink some more. To my left, a younger couple shares a plate of something fried, sizing each other up and talking confidentially. A second or third date, most likely. Will it last?

I order, in broken Japanese, a plate of grilled eel. It does not disappoint; even the bones seem to melt away.

Someone sits down next to me. It's a guy, around my age. In fact, he looks a lot like me— black hair just a little too long, round features, clean shaven. However, the resemblance ends there. I don't like his energy: he's wearing a leather jacket, elbows on the counter like he owns the place. He orders something hard and gestures imperiously at the bartender, like a low-level mobster. I groan. Fuck this guy.

I do my best to ignore him, but he starts singing to himself— an obnoxious, tuneless drone. This is, in my opinion, the worst kind of person: the root cause of war and conjugal violence. Every time he walks into a room, the doomsday clock ticks one minute closer to midnight.

When the man finally turns to me, I'm already visualizing my escape. But it's too late. I utter a chilly *sumimasen* and inform him that while I may look like everyone else in here, my home is worlds away. If this leaves any impression on him, though, he doesn't show it. He continues talking past me in brittle Japanese, downing drinks faster than I can count. The couple sitting on my other side get up and leave, catching a nervous glance at my companion on their way out.

The guy is still talking. I don't know what he's saying, but his tone speaks for itself. It's like listening to opera in a foreign language; when we don't understand the words, we're free to enjoy the raw emotion of sound. The clipped staccato of his gesticulations reminds me of piano music— something modern, borderline experimental. An angry sonata, a study in bitterness. I nod my head at random intervals.

Finally, he says, in English:

"You like sing karaoke?"

I shake my head emphatically.

"No, sorry. It's not for me."

He swears— or so it appears— and slams his glass down on the countertop. It's then that I notice the missing finger. I try to look away, but he's caught me staring. His smile says, so are you gonna ask me what happened to my finger or what? I have no intention of asking this question, but I already know the answer. We both know what's going on here. There's no need to speak, because everything reads plainly in our expressions; and we're five moves ahead like a game of chess.

At this point, the music fades out and someone new takes the stage. It's a stooped old woman, wearing what looks like a fishing hat. Grateful for a distraction, I turn around. She takes the microphone and says a few words, to scattered applause. Then, she brings the mic stand over to the upright piano, adjusts the height, and sits down at the keys. The backing track comes on, and a sentimental piano introduction plays from the recording before easing into melody. At this point, the woman takes over on the upright piano and begins to sing.

It's not an especially good performance— in fact, the woman's voice is squeaky and shrill. But she's really going for it. Despite the crooked phrases and lines off-key, an authentic feeling comes through. Technique aside, there's something arresting about her delivery; like the raw spontaneity of a grainy cell phone photo. Fuck autotune, I think to myself in wonder. The words are foreign to me, but it matters little. The rest of the clientele are held in rapture.

The song ends, the woman's voice cracking slightly on the final note. As the karaoke track fades out, the room erupts in applause, customers nodding in unanimous approval and delight. I join in, clapping feverishly— genuinely moved by this offbeat performance. When I turn back to my drinks, I'm shocked to see my thuggish bar mate wiping his eyes, red with emotion. Upon seeing me, he immediately tries to conceal this display of weakness with a snarl. The atmosphere— briefly spellbound— falls back to earth. Some inoffensive jazz fades in, and the chatter resumes.

The barmaid walks over and removes my empty plate, scraped clean but for a couple of stray bones. Then, between shots of whisky, the man says:

"You like... girls?"

I cock my eyebrow.

"Depends on the girl."

"I find girl for you. You pay."

"Excuse me?"

Then:

"You Chinese?"

"No."

He says something I don't catch. Then he pulls out what looks like a business card and shows it to me. It's covered with pornographic headshots of young girls, barely legal. I get the picture, and I'm not interested.

"Listen. I get the picture, but I'm not interested, okay?"

"Where you stay?"

"It doesn't matter. Look, I've gotta get going—"

Seizing my chance, I take out my wallet and place a few bills on the counter. Normally, I would ask the bartender to keep the change and be on my way; but here, I was told, people don't tip. So I wait a tense few seconds while the barmaid counts my coins, caught in the stare of this pushy lowlife from Fukushima. In my peripheral vision, I see him glaring, devious thoughts churning violently behind his ugly face. Finally, it's done, and I can leave. I nod without smiling, slip off the barstool and head for the exit. My unsavory friend follows me with his gaze, all the way to the door.

Once I'm outside, I shut my eyes and take the night air through my nose. Fecund aromas waft across the road from the adjacent shoreline. It's getting late, but I don't feel like sleeping just yet. Buzzed from the sake and lazily introspect, the thrill of the unknown suddenly hits me in full; I'm completely alone in this town, with no friends or clients, no utility bills, no grudges, no history. I'm at the opera: pulled into a foreign story I can't follow, unfettered by meaning and the burden of language; the sounds and the set are perfectly abstract. Anything could happen here.

Anything could happen here.

That's the last thought I have before something hard smashes against the back of my head.

*

When I come to, someone's dragging me across a cold, slippery floor. It's pitch dark, and they've got me by the ankles. The back of my hands slide across a smooth and slightly wet surface.

They dump me in an undisclosed location, and then leave. I hear their footsteps growing distant, echoing through what must be some kind of corridor. Then the sound dies out altogether, leaving a troubled silence. Instinctively, I reach for my pockets; my phone and wallet are gone. There's no sign of my camera bag either. I try sitting up, but a searing pain shoots through my head. Unable to rise, I simply lie there and wait for the throbbing to subside. From the corner of my eye, I see a pair of windows, moonlight casting the walls in pale blue. Everything is wet and clammy. I can't see it, but I seem to be lying in a pool of water; my limbs and back are being slowly soaked through.

It must have been that gangster. Unhinged— and offended that I declined his intriguing offer— he followed me into the street, knocked me out, and stole my valuables before driving me to some remote dumping ground and leaving me there. The scene is all too plausible, and I groan at my own carelessness. Whatever city-boy swagger I'd possessed before this was now exposed as a fragile, laughable farce. Twenty-five years of streetwise living? Give me a break.

There's an acrid stink in the air— mold and rubbish. It's a familiar smell, reaching me from the halls of memory. Where's the connection? The back of my head sloshes in a dirty puddle. Then I understand.

I've been here before.

The girl is here, too.

She's lying a few feet away, breathing softly. In the moonlight, I recognize her face; this is the place, beyond any doubt. Dreams cross into wakefulness, flickering noiselessly between tangible and intangible states. I reach out and touch her arm; it's cold and limp.

Then the music starts. It seems to come from everywhere at once, the familiar chords striking like gongs. The notes fall together like water droplets, sparse at first but increasingly agitated; soon, they're all around us, dropping in heavy clusters. I tighten my grip on the woman's wrist; I need to keep her here, on this side. She's the key to the madness; a figment of that other place.

Whole minutes have passed before I notice that she's becoming transparent. Not only her: my hand and forearm are disappearing too. I can see the floor straight through my fading skin. I've lost sensation in my hand and arm— I can no longer move them. I cry out; my voice is swallowed by the rising cacophony. I roll over and try to rip myself free with my other hand, but it passes right through, slamming the hard ground underneath. *Please,* I croak. *Stay here. Stay here with me.* It's spreading up my arm and down my shoulder; what will happen when my heart becomes transparent? I find out moments later. As the emptiness passes over the chest cavity where that vital organ resides, my terror suddenly goes mute. I watch the rest of my body vanishing, feeling only a slow-motion indifference. It's crawling up my neck, now; soon, it'll consume my eyes and brain. It's okay. After all, this life happens just once, but dreams last forever in their nonexistence. So few things are true and real, on this side, but the number of imaginary worlds keeps expanding into infinity. The woman smiles through strands of mangled black hair, nearly gone.

Then, before I disappear, it all falls into place. How could I have missed it? It was so obvious, so elementary, the whole time. Distracted, and misled by an unsentimental heart, the metaphor had passed before me in plain sight. The epiphany sends a tremor through what's left of my material body. From this moment, even in my numb, fading state, I experience perfect lucidity: I renounce, completely, the literal universe and pledge my remaining thoughts to the immaterial. It's almost time: my eyes go first, and then my ears. The music stops. For an instant, there is only pure consciousness: the primordial awareness of being, free of all sensation.

*

```
Dear X,

    Thank you for your message. At this time, the
piano in question is no longer in Mr. Sakamoto's
possession and we are not at liberty to divulge
the identity of its current owner. Our apologies
for this.
```

However, Mr. Sakamoto would like you to know that as a matter of historic record, the site where the piano was first recovered in Fukushima has been demolished in the years following the 2011 nuclear incident. The original schoolhouse is no longer there.

Best wishes in your endeavors.

Celia Horowitz

*

> Hey

> How are you doing?

> I tried calling you earlier, but it went straight to voicemail. Not sure if you're still in Fukushima

> Things got a bit complicated, I think I'm going to stay here with Keiji. I'm changing my flight, or canceling it I don't know yet. I know this might hurt you, and I'm sorry about that

> These things are difficult

> :(

> I think it's best if we don't talk anymore.

> Let me know if you're ok

> P.S. I showed my boyfriend some of your photos, he was really impressed!

> Oops, I don't know why I said that. Not really helpful.

> I'm a little tipsy ATM

> In the bathroom

> Oh god I don't know what I want. You're sweet but

> I need to sort things out

> I hope your figuring out your shit here in Fukushima

> Maybe we can see each other when I get back, might be a while though

> Bye now.

*

It's daybreak. A crow is pecking on my shoulder, mistaking me for a carcass. The pain stirs me awake; I shudder, and the crow takes off.

I'm lying in an empty lot. It's quiet and overgrown, unruly weeds rising from the mounds of cracked cement. The sky is shifting from blue to orange. There's no room, no woman, no piano in sight. Just the debris of someone else's disaster.

I'm still here.

But for how long?

*

The sun has reached high noon before I regain my strength. I stand up, straining against a painful vertigo. I make my way across the empty lot, battered remains crumbling underfoot.

There's a path through the trees, and I follow it. Eventually, I come to some kind of clearing that opens into a field, and then a road. A single car drives by, the driver staring me down but not slowing. I watch it until it disappears around a bend. Without a phone or map, I'm not sure where to go.

I decide to follow the road, heading in the same direction as the car that passed me by, led by only a vague hope that I'll end up back in town. My pants and sweater are smeared with mud; every step sends a spasm of pain up my spine to the back of my head.

Somehow, I make it back into town. I was never very far to begin with, it turns out. I recognize a 7-Eleven by the side of the road, and from there it's a short walk back to my hostel. The Cherry Bar is still there, closed until nightfall.

I manage to communicate the basic outline of my ordeal to the receptionist, who then calls management and guides me through the process of making a police report. With admirable presence of mind, I leave out the most riveting part of my story— the only part that really matters. What I don't understand— something the police cannot answer— is why I was allowed to remain here, on this side of the chasm. I suspect that only one person can answer that question.

Fortunately, I'd left my passport and some spare cash in my room. I pack my things and ask the front desk where I can use the internet; they direct me to a communal rec room equipped with two desktop computers. From there, I pull up the relevant windows and make a few calls to my bank and cell phone provider. Luckily, they're able to cancel my credit cards before any serious fraud is committed. I try to check my emails, but the login demands confirmation via text message; without a phone, I'm stuck. Moving on, I decide to book a flight back home for the following day— I figure I'll explain everything to Soren after the fact. After all, she's here with someone. As for me, there's no reason to stick around.

Everything is arranged. I leave my email address with the reception desk, just in case the cops somehow manage to recover my stolen possessions. But I have little hope, and it doesn't matter much to me either way. As far as I'm concerned, they're now lost to the currents of chaos.

I leave Fukushima that same afternoon. The bullet train whisks me back to Tokyo, and I eat an egg salad sandwich I picked up at the 7-Eleven. I periodically examine my hand — the one that touched her— and check it for any lingering transparency. For the time being, it appears to be made of flesh.

My overnight in Tokyo is a simple affair. I take a lonely walk around Shinjuku, fend off the advances of several gay bar hosts, and eat a plate of fast food curry. Without my camera or phone, these moments are captured and engraved in memory— that most fallible of renderings. The streets are lurid and alien, a photographer's dream; even so, now's not the right time— there's something I need to do. I return to my accommodations for the evening: a single pod in a room with eight other bunk beds. The beds are packed together like a beehive, each person afforded a single capsule of privacy. I crawl inside, turn off the lights and curl up in the sheets, not bothering to remove my clothes. Tomorrow, will we all emerge as butterflies?

*

When I finally return to the City, much sooner than anticipated, everything is just as it was. I'd left Tokyo after dark, and it's nighttime when I arrive here, on the other side of a manic, spinning planet. The airport is quiet and grim; a few maintenance workers set about their thankless duties, sweeping the floors beside long-closed restaurant kiosks. Nothing is open, except for a McDonald's.

Where are you coming from?

Fukushima. I mean, Tokyo.

What were you doing over there?

Just visiting with a friend.

Oh yeah? Like, a girlfriend?

Yeah. Something like that.

And she didn't come back with you?

Nope. Not this time.

[Slides passport through a scanner]

That's a shame.

I guess so, yeah.

[...]

How long were you over there for?

Um, three days.

Three days?! That's a real short trip to go so far.

Yeah. But I had to come back for an assignment. Couldn't be helped.

Ok. What do you do for work, sir?

I'm a photographer.

What kind of photography do you do?

Mostly portraits. Like, headshots and stuff. I try to bring out the best in people.

[Sizing me up] So where's your camera then?

I uh, I didn't bring it on this trip. I wasn't working— I just wanted to see the sights.

Mhmm. And where's home for you?

Home?

Yeah. Where do you live.

Right. Sorry I'm just— I'm jet lagged.

[Rubs eyes, takes a deep breath]

My home's in _____.

That right?

[Stares blankly] Yeah, that's right.

What are you bringing back with you?

Nothing. I actually have less now than I did before.

[Looks up] What do you mean.

[Clearing throat nervously] Oh, I just mean I left something over there. A gift for my friend.

But you're not bringing anything back with you now?

No. I guess not.

So you don't have anything to declare?

[Thinking it over] No... Nope, nothing.

[Frowning suspiciously] Nothing?

[Squirming] Nothing. Nothing to declare.

[The agent eyes me dubiously. Finally, he stamps my passport and hands it back to me without making eye contact.]

Have a good night.

Thanks.

And welcome back.

[...]

Thank you.

*

She's practicing her scales. I hear them before I even open my door; up, down, up, down. The moon swells and recedes, elections come and go, rent is paid on the first of the month. Cycles remain intact, hurtling toward some kind of eternity.

As soon as I enter my apartment, however, the scales abruptly cease. I throw down my bag and suitcase and stand completely still, listening. No sound, no music. I close my eyes and exhale very, very slowly.

*

"I'll do it."

She's preparing a pot of tea. The kettle is whistling, but she doesn't seem to notice. I turn off the stove for her.

We're sitting opposite one another at her kitchen table, steam rising from two cups of heavily caffeinated tea.

"Thanks for inviting me in. Um, your houseplants are looking better. They were a bit dry before."

"No time to water."

"That's alright. They're stronger than they look."

There's nothing else to say, so I quickly dispense with the pleasantries.

"Anyway. I think you know why I'm back early, don't you?"

She stares at my teacup with a grave expression.

"I'm sorry I didn't understand at the time. About the piano, I mean. It was too soon— I didn't know what you meant."

I blow across the top of my cup.

"But I know now. At least, I think I do."

My neighbor nods, but avoids my gaze.

"I saw *her* in Fukushima."

I take a sip of tea. It's scalding hot; I can barely taste it.

"That night you found me here, in your apartment, that was the first time I saw her. You must have known that. Why didn't you say anything?"

Anxious, I reach instinctively for my pocket; but it is, of course, empty.

"They wouldn't tell me what happened to the piano— the drowned piano. I know Sakamoto had it, but now it's somewhere else.

"It's here, isn't it?"

My neighbor is staring straight at me, now.

"I just want you to know: she's still alive. She's halfway between this world and that *other place*, but part of her lives here. You can hear her when you play that piano. But if you want to see her..."

Her eyes are fixed on me like a telescope pointing at some distant planet. I clear my throat.

"I won't say too much more about it. Whatever happened in Fukushima, that's your business. But...

I want to be of assistance, in any way I can. If I take your picture, maybe— maybe I can get her in the frame. We need to bring her back from that *other place*.

It's presumptuous of me, maybe. I'm not the best photographer. But I would like this chance."

I tap my foot nervously. My neighbor's gaze is unyielding.

"The problem is, my camera got stolen by a gangster. So I'll have to get a new one. If you can wait a few days...

Maybe it's out of line for me to say this—

But there's still time.

Whenever you're ready, I'll do it."

A long silence hangs between us. While I wait for an answer, time speeds up, rewinds and runs in mad circles; a girl waits in limbo for the rest of her to follow, or pull her back; someone from the other side cries foul, holding the balance of lives lost against those yet to come; and through it all, a world of genius and drowned pianos skirts the liminal edge of folly, and beauty.

4′33′′

He woke up that morning to a frozen world.

His alarm clock read 4:33 AM, a time corroborated by the barely-blue sky outside his bedroom window. But it didn't *feel* so early. In fact, he felt distinctly overslept, wracked by the kind of anxiety that precedes a missed flight. He'd been awakened by an unpleasant sound— the sputtering engine of a truck on the street below. He turned over and tried to go back to sleep, but it was too late. A fast-fading dream grew distant, replaced by a litany of troubles. Resigned, the man groaned and slid over the edge of his bed, not bothering to straighten the sheets.

Dawn is a mostly silent layover from night into day. The man stumbled over to his kitchen— a mere three steps from his bed, this being a studio apartment— and put on some hot water for coffee, leaving the kettle to simmer on the two-burner hotplate that figured as some kind of stove. He owned two mugs: one for him, and another for some future companion. For the time being, he used both himself.

The coffee was old and slightly burnt: just as he liked it. Today was an "A" day— meaning, he drank from Mug A, the one with his high school's official crest printed on the side. It was a freebie from the Alumnae Association, one he'd taken home as a joke to himself in a moment of irony. These days, he struggled to remember what was ironic about it.

The sun was starting to break out over the horizon, signaling a beginning for those willing to give life another go. Finishing his coffee, the man placed his mug in the sink and left it there, running the tap for a perfunctory rinse but stopping short of properly washing it out. Then he went to the bathroom, brushed his teeth, and took a quick shower. There was a problem with the pipes: the "warm" setting unleashed an alternating flow of cold and hot water, strictly segregated, all but failing to blend together. Taking a shower in this apartment meant getting frostbitten and scalded by the same stream of water. It was like running the heat and air conditioning at the same time, turning up one dial to negate the other in a mad game of escalation. *Like nuclear proliferation,* the man thought moodily as he scrubbed shampoo into his hair.

Once he was dressed and feeling reasonably alert, he dropped to the floor and did a few pushups next to his bed, counting painfully up to twenty-seven repetitions. A pain in his left elbow prevented him from continuing any further, so he rounded up to thirty and called it a morning. Then he took out his phone and checked the news. Nothing of much importance— that's what he told himself every time he scanned the headlines, whose nakedly biased reportage seemed to cast the world in darkening shades of bleakitude. Collapsing ecosystems and political acrimony competed for the attention of a world-weary populace, painting something like apocalypse wallpaper.

The first signs were subtle. That the clock on his cell phone continued to indicate 4:33 AM despite all evidence to the contrary, did not cause him any distress— he wrote this off as a technical error, one of those esoteric problems best handled by people making six-figures out in California. The neighbors were unusually quiet, too: at least *someone* could be counted on to pace their apartment at this hour, whether the early risers or the all-night insomniacs. But then again, who was he to say? It was Sunday, after all.

But when he left his building and hit the streets in search of breakfast, he knew something was wrong. The ambient sounds— traffic, chatter, the rattle of subways— had been altered somehow. There were no cars driving down the road, but there appeared to be a handful of accidents; a three-car collision near a fire hydrant down the street, and a cab that had driven into a streetlamp. One vehicle— a garbage truck— was double parked right in front of the man's apartment building. This is the truck that woke me up, the man thought to himself. But that doesn't make any sense, does it? That was over two hours ago.

A closer look revealed a disturbing sight. The young guy hanging off the back of the truck— a customary sight for those who've spent time observing garbage trucks and sanitation workers— was frozen in place. Completely motionless. One hand held onto the metal handle beside the garbage compactor while the other gripped the rim of a plastic bin. He looked to be halfway through a round of dumping: the garbage bin was tilted just slightly, a black trash bag poking out near the top. But the guy wasn't moving. He looked like a wax figurine from Madame Tussauds; not a single twitch or quiver in his entire body.

The man, reflexively, began to shout at the young sanitation worker.

"Hey, hello? Are you okay? What's going on?"

He waved his hand in front of the young worker's face, which was partially obscured by a pair of sunglasses. No reaction. The man reached out and tapped the sanitation worker on the shoulder; fleshy and real. But still, no reaction. Stiff as a corpse.

The man staggered back, edged around to the front of the truck and peered in through the driver's seat window. The driver was there— but he, too, was immobilized, caught in the act of lighting a cigarette. It protruded from his mouth at a comic angle, his eyes bulging. The man banged on the window, to no avail.

"Hi, excuse me— *hello!* Can you hear me? *HELLO.*"

Failing to elicit a response, the man backed away and set off down the sidewalk. As he turned the corner, he almost collided with a well-dressed woman in heels. Like the two garbage disposal workers, she was completely inanimate. The man gave a yelp, ducked out of the way, looked back, and ran down the street to the end of the block.

Everywhere he went, it was the same. Ordinary citizens, early morning hustlers, turned into statues. From the corner cop to the street sweeper, no one was spared; the latter could be observed with their hands around a broom handle, earbud cables dangling listlessly around their neck. The rubber wires swayed in the breeze while their owner stared doggedly at a crushed soda can by the curb as if transfixed, their arms stuck in mid-sweep. In a spasm of frustration, the man kicked the can, sending it clattering down the pavement; no comment from the sidewalk cleaner, or anyone else. A few pigeons waddled about and picked at clumps of litter; they, it seemed, were unaffected. The man looked at them helplessly.

"Do you guys know what's going on? Is there some disease going around?"

The pigeons, for their part, played dumb.

"Great. Fantastic. Thanks for nothing, you dirty chickens."

Cars were stopped in the middle of the road, their drivers glued to the steering wheels. Crossing the street to his local twenty-four hour deli, the man strode inside and surveyed the scene. The owner— a steely grandmother from the outskirts of Busan, Korea— was midway through serving a cup of coffee to a burly construction worker, her hand outstretched, stiff as a mannequin. The coffee looked cold and sludgy, a few hours old. Miserably, the man paced the length of the deli. Then he grabbed a box of oversized croissants, lay a five dollar bill on the counter, and left the shop in a daze.

He clomped down the street and ate a croissant without enthusiasm, tossing a few crumbs to another gang of pigeons— so far, the only creatures still moving. A vagrant lay on a spread of cardboard boxes in front of a pharmacy. It must have been nearly 8 o'clock, but most shops appeared to be closed, and the streets were strangely empty. A digital display above a bus stop read 4:33 AM. The man took out his phone to check: 4:33 AM. How could this be? He opened his internet browser and searched "current time". Same result. A quick glance at the news confirmed it: there were no headlines or articles posted after 4:33 AM., the last update bearing a time stamp of half past three. It was as if everything had just stopped dead in the middle of the night without any warning. He dialed his father, and then a woman he'd met online a few months back: both times, it rang out without any response. Then he tried 9-1-1, Verizon, Citibank— nothing. He imagined the nondescript, harshly-lit offices and overnight workers frozen in their chairs, unable to answer the ringing telephone. Could they even hear it? Were they dead, or alive? Or neither? Just simply, frozen?

Clearly, something had happened at 4:33. Human activity across the city had abruptly ceased without explanation. Time itself was behaving nonsensically, even under the most outlandish interpretations of quantum theory; the clocks had stopped, but the day continued to open. A full sun lit the streets from the east, unfettered by clouds or the mysterious pause which had the entire city— and maybe the world— trapped in suspended animation. And the birds kept picking dirty breadcrumbs from the sidewalk.

The man was running now, scanning the quiet streets for signs of movement. He tore down a residential lane, banging on the first floor and half basement apartment windows facing the sidewalk.

Hello? Is anyone awake? Can you hear me? HELP! SAY SOMETHING FOR FUCK'S SAKE.

Back on the commercial drag, another homeless person lay wedged in the doorway of a boarded-up storefront. The man shouted at him, restraining the urge to kick the unlucky hobo in the head.

"I know you're awake, you motherfucker! I know you can hear me! Get up— don't pretend— this isn't *funny*, you understand? This isn't fucking *funny!*"

Scenes of mild carnage— crashed cars, trucks on sidewalks— were juxtaposed with frozen traffic; intersections half-crossed, red lights partially run. Some vehicles had run wild, while others had simply frozen in place. The result was a collage of still images from some documentary film; one of those urban rhapsodies by a broke yet critically acclaimed arthouse director you've never heard of. And now, a nowhere man caught in the action had become the film's unwitting subject.

The man was frightened. Not because he was so very alone— solitude was nothing new— but because the anonymity found in heaving crowds had suddenly been dashed, leaving him at the center of a conspiracy; something cooked up by the neutrinos and poorly-understood particles bouncing around a cheeky universe. Every time he passed another frozen body, he half expected it to spring to life— foaming at the mouth, ready to tear him to bits. That he remained animate was little consolation; it only drew attention to his otherwise inconspicuous existence, which he preferred to keep discreet. He imagined a hidden camera— an aerial drone, following his frantic movements across the neighborhood from above, broadcasting his plight to an audience somewhere. The scrutiny was unbearable.

The man ducked into the 83rd Avenue Subway station, narrowly avoiding a sewer rat on his way down. A couple of fare-evading teenagers blocked the turnstiles mid-jump while the ticket booth attendant stared listlessly through the glass; a trickle of runoff from the street above dripped down the walls, pooling by the base of an out-of-service ticket dispenser, a crushed cigarette butt floating on the surface. The man swiped his MetroCard— mostly to check if that particular mechanism still worked here; it did, with a reassuring click and a beep. He pushed through the turnstiles and headed for the platform below.

The station was deserted. Several meters underground, out of reach from the sun, it felt very much like 4:33 AM, this timestamp flashing across an electronic display panel halfway down the platform. The man paced the length of the station from one end to the other, checking for signs of life and peering down into the tunnels.

"This is my painting."

The man spun around. A person of indeterminate ethnicity and androgynous features was walking along the platform some twenty feet away. She— or he, more likely *they*— appeared to be moving normally; marvelously animate, and unhurried. Like a younger Tilda Swinton, but with dark hair and coffee cream skin. Their trench coat swung above a pair of black combat boots probably gleaned from a second hand shop.

"How do you like it?"

The mysterious figure stopped, and smiled.

"Hi! I didn't expect to see anyone. Anyone who wasn't, you know, frozen. I guess that was my mistake. Can't be helped, I guess. I'm not perfect."

The man blurted out:

"What?"

"This is one of my new pieces, obviously. More of a work in progress, to tell you the truth. But not bad for a first draft."

"Are you high? Have you *seen* what's going on? Are we the only ones who aren't frozen?"

"Oh. Probably. Hard to know— I haven't really looked it over properly."

The man scratched the outside of his ear and frowned unhappily. *Perfect*, he thought miserably. *Everything's fucked, and I'm stuck with Andy Warhol here.*

"I'm Ash, by the way."

"Hi."

"You don't do names?"

"No, I do have one."

"Well? What is it?"

Grudgingly, the man gave his name.

"A-*ha*. Very nice to meet you."

"*Enchanté.*"

Ash took a few paces forward, prompting the man to step out of the way.

"Should we sit?"

They took a seat on a dirty wooden bench near the center of the platform. The man kept his hands in his pockets, fidgeting restlessly.

"I'll be honest with you. I have no idea what you're talking about, and my head hurts. Something is very wrong here, but you don't seem to think so. Care to let me in on the joke?"

"Oh, it's no joke. This isn't meant to be a satirical piece. Though I guess you *could* look at it that way, couldn't you?"

The person named Ash folded their arms. The man struggled to respond, clicking his teeth but saying nothing.

"I'm sorry, I know I'm being ridiculous. I'd better explain myself."

"Please do."

"I'm a painter."

"Yeah, I got that."

"And this is my painting."

"*What* is your painting?"

The painter stretched out their arms and opened their palms to the empty subway station.

"All of *this*. The stillness. The current weirdness."

"You mean..."

The man cleared his throat.

"— you mean *you did this?*"

The painter shrugged apologetically.

"It's not really finished. Like, I have to keep working on it."

"I don't understand. You froze everyone?"

The painter checked their watch— an Apple Watch.

"We used to tell time on our watches, but now they do pretty much everything *except* tell time. Strange, isn't it?"

The man had no opinion on the matter.

"Hey, we're around the same age, right? When were you born?"

"1993."

"Dead on. Me too."

The man failed to grasp the significance of this connection.

"I call this piece *4' 33"*. If you had to classify it, I'd say it's a still life."

The display panel above the platform continued to indicate 4:33 AM.

"So it really *was* you? You stopped all the clocks?"

"Well, I named it after a piece of music by John Cage. Have you heard of him? Or are you more of a Top 40 kinda guy?"

"Uh..."

"Top 40 then. That's okay. *4' 33"* is a famous composition. Anyone can perform it. You get your musicians together, start the clock, and shut up for exactly four minutes and thirty-three seconds. Nobody plays anything— you just listen. The random sounds around you — people breathing, traffic, the wind— *that* becomes the music. Do you see what I mean?

So I wanted to create something— like a kind of *hommage* to *4' 33"*. A concept piece where people just stop— completely— and feel the world around them, without their interference."

This explanation went completely beyond the man's limited knowledge of modern art. The two sat without speaking, listening to the low hum of the subway tunnels. Then, the man said:

"You're crazy."

But he knew the painter named Ash spoke some kind of truth.

"So all those people... they're still alive?"

"Oh, yeah, of course they are. I'm not *that* messed up— I'm no fan of the apocalypse. They're alive, for sure."

"And you're going to unfreeze them?"

Instead of answering, the painter continued:

"Do you have any heroes? Who inspires you?"

"Um, that's tough to say. I guess I like Bruce Lee."

"Bruce Lee. Good answer. Anyone more recent? Like, someone our own age?"

The man thought about this. There seemed no alternative but to follow the painter's elliptical line of questioning. But try as he might, he struggled to come up with an answer.

"I don't know. I can't think of anyone *that* special."

He started to rattle off a few names— pop stars, entrepreneurs, activists— but the painter cut in.

"Exactly. There's nobody. No cataclysmic personality for us to rally around and call our spokesperson. We're a mess, spread out across the internet and whatever trendy cities will take us in for a few months before we move on to the next cool place. We don't have our Beatles, Michael Jackson, Rosa Parks, or Bruce Lee— people who transcended their own generation and never looked back. The closest thing we've got is Harry Potter, and those people *aren't even real.* Doesn't that say something about us?"

The man nodded in dumb acknowledgment, alarmed at the painter's excitable rhetoric.

"I've always felt like we're transitional— between big things, with none to call our own. Our fashion is nonexistent, our music is garbage, our movies are boring, and nobody reads books anymore. Our food is pretty good, but that's about it."

The painter clicked their tongue.

"Huh, I'll have to think about the food thing. Maybe that's what will save us, funnily enough."

The man reached into his pocket and checked his phone, for no reason other than that it was there.

"I'm not an especially talented painter. And there's absolutely no money in it unless you teach at an art school. But I wanted to make something that was *ours*. Something that would last, something for posterity; a kind of emblem or anthem. It's not crafty, or original. But I had to do it. This is for us."

The painter named Ash again raised their arm in a sweeping motion, gesturing toward the soot-covered ceilings of the 83rd Street station like a monarch laying claim to all the land. Their long trench coat seemed to flap around their shoulders like a triumphant cape in the wind.

"This is our legacy. Conquering time so we don't have to grow up. The rest of the world won't wait, as you can see, but at least *we* can hit the pause button on this thing called life. Beautiful, isn't it? I think it's my best work."

Suddenly, the painter leaned over and kissed the man passionately. Caught completely off guard, the man stiffened, then relaxed. He closed his eyes, and thought of nothing at all.

When they broke off from one another, a faint rumbling could be heard from deep in the tunnels. Soft at first, it mounted in volume until the familiar headlights of a train shone through the obscurity at the end of the platform and lit up the dirty tiles on the wall. It pulled into the station and came to a shuddering halt in front of them. The painter smiled, but made no move to stand up.

"This is your train."

They motioned toward the doors, which flew open as if on cue. The man obediently stood up, looking uncertainly from the train to the painter who sat with one leg over the other.

"Where am I going?"

"Now *that's* what I call legacy," said the painter named Ash, beaming.

The man walked forward a few paces, stepped onto the train, and turned to face the platform. Then the doors abruptly closed. As if roused from a trance, the man's eyes widened, and he put his palm against the window.

"Wait! Why me?"

The painter waved, and the train pulled away.

It was certainly moving, though not very quickly.

For four minutes and thirty-three seconds,

A lone passenger listened for clarity

Unsure if he'd left it behind him

Or if it was so far ahead

As to be practically behind again.

When the time was up

He left the compartment and stepped out into a world still frozen

All was quiet.

Not even the angst of a generation

Could shake the silence

Because it was so perfect.

Acknowledgments

I would like to thank Derek and Colton for opening the door for me, and showing me through it. I want to thank my family, Ruby, Bobby, and Ming. Thank you to Sahara, for always believing in me and indulging my imaginary worlds. Thank you to Cindy and Patrick, for your bottomless hospitality. Thank you to Chelsea and Derek for your sharp-eyed editing. Lastly, I would like to thank all of my friends, from the beginning to the present moment; thank you for the best of times, and so many memories.

Other RCN Media Titles

Just Being Human
by Colton Nelson

Rough Diamond
by Derek Hanebury

A Kind of Seeing
by Shelley Penner

King of Dhamma
by Huei Lin

The Fifth Planet
by Joan Jedy

Responsive
by Colton Nelson

Double Cross
by Joan Jedy

Ms. Holliman's Employer
by Laura Sturgeon

Brother's of the Heart
by Shelley Penner

Both Sides Now
by Derek Hanebury, Libbie Morin & Vicki Drybrough

Alberni Aquarium Cookbook
by The Alberni Valley

Haven Hold
by Shelley Penner

Something Else Altogether
by Derek Hanebury

Afraid of Heights
by Joan Jedy

A Nickel a Bucket
by Laura Sturgeon

KIDS Books

The Adventures of Bob and Avery Series:
By Kay J Douglas & Eric Gardiner
1. Bob and Avery Help Helga The Witch
2. Bob and Avery Go to Space
3. Untitled 3rd Bob and Avery Adventure

By Gail Morton
1. Two Weeks With Charlie
2. The Giving Raven
3. Rockfish

More coming soon
**To see a complete list go to:
www.rcn.media/books**

Recommended by the Publisher

Brothers of the Heart:
By Shelley Penner

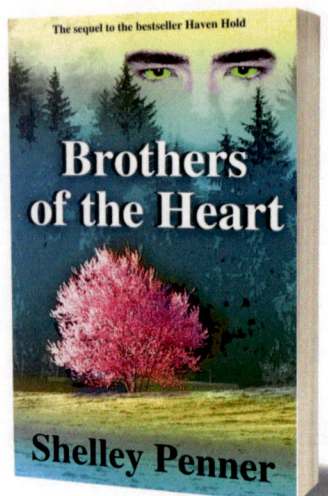

This is the sequel to the best-selling Haven Hold by Shelley Penner. When Zach McKenna arrives at Haven Hold, his self-esteem is dismally low. Having lost his entire family to vicious raiders, he feels an intense distrust of mutants. Despite hearing of the holders' friendship with the mutant, Daniel, the first time he sees Daniel, Zach shoots him and rouses the anger of the entire hold. Will they still allow him to stay, or will they exile him to make his way through the dangerous wilderness alone? As a mutant born amongst normals, Daniel has suffered rejection, isolation and betrayal. When the people of Haven Hold offer him a permanent place in their community, it seems a dream come true. But can he teach Zach, his new partner, to trust a mutant?

Find out more & get a free preview at
www.HavenHold.net

AVAILABLE WHEREVER BOOKS ARE SOLD
Signed editions available at www.rcn.media

*Amazon Canada